HIS TASTE OF TEMPTATION

CATHRYN FOX

COPYRIGHT

Discover other titles by Cathryn Fox at www.cathrynfox.com. Please sign up for Cathryn's Newsletter for freebies, ebooks, news and contests:
https://app.mailerlite.com/webforms/landing/c1f8n1

ISBN 978-1-928056-57-7
Print ISBN 978-1-928056-74-4

1

Just when she thought her morning couldn't get any worse.

Madison Graham let out a sputtering yelp. Unfortunately, with a stuffed-up nose and well on her way to a major case of laryngitis, it came out sounding more like a Pekinese dog's yappy bark rather than the desperate cry of a woman in need of help.

"What the hell," a sleepy voice grumbled from behind her. "Ah, shit. Not again."

With her hand inside the hole in the wall that had yet to be fixed since their last plumbing disaster, Madison cupped her palm over the end of the broken pipe, struggling to stem the water flow before it did any more damage to her bathroom, or worse, leak through to her bakery on the ground floor below. Shooting a frantic glance over her shoulder, she saw Jonah Crosby, her childhood best friend and current roommate, and gave an aggravated shake of her head.

"I really need to find a new place to live." Twisting around, Madison quickly switched hands on the pipe, gasping when another spurt of water shot into her face.

With his hands braced against the door facing, Jonah made a leisurely survey of the scene. "Or you could try taking a shower the way the rest of us do—inside the stall." Dressed in a pair of low hanging pajama pants that exposed a long, lean torso and those well-defined, V-shaped lats that attracted women in droves, Jonah gave her a crooked grin. His gaze skimmed over Madison's water-spattered glasses, then drifted downward, lingering on her thin nightshirt. Madison followed the direction of his glance and noticed that her nightshirt had been transformed into a prize-winning wet T-shirt after being hosed down by the broken water pipe.

"Seriously, Jonah, I need to get a better place."

Jonah cleared his throat. "Ah, you should probably get changed first," he teased.

"And you've got ten seconds to move," she warned, her teeth chattering as she repositioned her grip, ready to aim the spray Jonah's way. "Otherwise, you're next."

"Right. I'm on it." He disappeared from the doorway and hurried down the steep steps. A loud clang and few curses later, the gushing water trickled to a drip before coming to a full stop. Madison stepped back, wiped the moisture from her glasses, and attempted to squeeze the droplets from her long, soggy hair.

The old floorboards creaked under Jonah's weight as he jogged back to the bathroom. He grabbed a big, fluffy towel from the hook on the door and tossed it her way. Keeping his bare feet out of the ever-expanding puddle, he stood in the hall and braced his hands on the overhead door frame.

He assessed the damage and pulled a disgruntled face, one that made him look young and more boyish than his twenty-five years and had her thoughts careening back to their playground days.

One eyebrow arched when he asked, "You want me to call or do you want to?"

Madison pressed the towel to her chest and blotted her cold cheeks with a corner, groaning as she fought off a sneeze. She was battling the summer cold of the century—during Austin's worst heat wave, nonetheless—and really wasn't in the mood to get into another shouting match with her landlord. Besides, she already knew how the scenario would play out. Over the phone he'd promise to come by right away, going so far as to ensure her he was practically on her front stoop. Past experiences, however, had taught her that he'd show up on her doorstep at his leisure, leaving her high and dry, or in this case, wet and sodden, for days on end.

"You'd better do it this time." She grabbed a couple of towels from the sliver of a linen closet and tossed them onto the flooded tile floor before adding, "Not that I think it will do any good."

Jonah tapped his fingers on the paint-chipped doorframe and nodded in agreement. "Maybe I should just call Brad. He'll know what to do."

At the mention of Jonah's older brother, a shiver moved through Madison, one that had little to do with the water chilling her feverish skin and everything to do with the hot hunk of military man who had been invading her dreams since her teen years.

"What would I know how to do?"

Jonah spun around. "Hey, bro. Just in time."

"What would I know?" Brad began again, but his words fell off. Madison glanced up, expecting to see him surveying the bathroom, only to find him looking directly at her breasts and the ample curves she spent years hiding. Her nipples tightened in response, unbridled desire moving into her quivering stomach as their gazes collided.

"We...uh...we had another flood," she managed to croak out, hoping she didn't sound as breathless as she felt.

"I can see that," he responded, his voice sounding tighter than normal.

Her blood pulsed hot when his smoldering gaze tracked a path down her body—a slow, lazy caress that instantly pushed back the cold inside her. Heat bombarded her as she became fully aware of her near-naked state—fully aware of what else Brad could *see*.

She snatched another towel from the closet and let it drop down in front of her as his gaze tracked back up her body and met hers. For a moment, she could almost swear there had been a flicker of interest backlighting his baby blues, but he gave a quick shake of his head and tore his gaze from hers. When he frowned and took in the sad state of her century-old bathroom, she knew she had to be mistaken. Guys like Brad didn't lust after girls like her. No, he was into vivacious, self-assured women. Brazen women who had it all and weren't afraid to use it to get what they wanted.

What he wasn't into were girls who spent the better part of their lives being called Fatty Maddy, along with a few other unkind names like S'mores Cracker.

Madison wrapped the towel around her chest and tucked it in, then reached for another to blot the water from her hair. It wasn't that she was fat, per se. She had been an early bloomer and had body image issues. She had worn oversized, bulky layers of clothing to cover her D-cup breasts and curvy hips, but rather than camouflaging her full figure, she had ended up looking like a big, round marshmallow. Sort of like a female version of the Michelin Man. That, of course, coupled with the last name Graham, was how the mean girls—and boys—from high school came up with the S'mores dig. God, teenagers really were the cruelest beings on earth—and, as far as she was concerned, not all that creative, either.

Size twelve boots splashed in the water as Brad stepped into the tight confines of the bathroom. Her pulse jumped in her throat as he leaned past her to look at the broken pipe. She tried to breathe in his familiar scent of fresh soap and clean skin, but her stuffed-up nose took that moment to run, gushing with the same enthusiasm as her broken pipe. Damn. She quickly reached for her box of tissue, only to find that it had become a casualty of faulty plumbing as well. In a very unattractive, unladylike move she sniffed hard, and, because the fate-Gods liked to kick her when she was down, Brad took that moment straighten to his full height and look directly at her.

Okay, her day had officially gone from bad to worse.

"Grab my toolbox from the truck," he said to Jonah, and that's when she realized he sounded as hoarse as she did, and that he was likely battling a cold too.

He folded his arms over his chest, the soft fabric of his T-shirt stretching across his broad shoulders. He took his time to inspect the damage, pulling the same disgruntled face that Jonah had earlier. Only on Brad, the expression was anything but boyish. Oh no, not at all. Here stood a *man*, ready to take charge, to do whatever was necessary to get the job done, and take all the time he needed to do it. A man who wasn't afraid to roll up his sleeves and get his hands dirty...or wet. It made him look hot and sexy and—good God, she needed to pull herself together!

Clearing her throat, Madison turned her thoughts to the two men in her life. Even though there was only two years between them, at twenty-seven, Brad was all man. One hundred percent grade-A male. The kind she wanted to serve up on a shiny platter and dive into with vigor. Hunger moved through her and she worked to find her voice as she finger combed her hair in some feeble attempt to make herself look presentable.

He shot a quick glance her way and a strange look came over his face, one she couldn't quite identify. "You...uh...you might want to get out of those wet clothes before you catch your death of cold." His turn of phrase reminded her of his late folks, his dad in particular.

"I've already got a cold," she mumbled, stepping onto one of the soaked towels. She pulled open the vanity drawer, grabbed her trusty lip balm, and applied it to her chapped lip. As the scent of cherry filled the air, she caught Brad wetting his own mouth, like he too was in need of relief.

"Want some?" She held the tube out to him. "It's cherry flavor, but it works."

His gaze dropped to her mouth, and then quickly darted away. "No," he bit out, his harsh tone surprising her.

She recapped the tube and tossed it back into her vanity. "What, you don't like cherry?"

The muscles along his jaw rippled. "I never said that."

Jonah came back with Brad's toolbox and she let the matter drop. Jonah stepped up beside his brother, and Madison smacked her lips to spread the balm. She couldn't help but compare the two men as they stood side by side. Where Brad was taller, with harder muscles and sharper features, Jonah was lean with a pretty-boy face. With his angelic attributes, Jonah would look at home on any Calvin Klein poster, although Madison couldn't help but wonder what his older brother would look like in those sexy designer underwear.

Along with his boyish good looks, Jonah was also easygoing, the life of the party and game for just about anything. Brad, on the other hand, was far more responsible. When his dad had died of lung disease after a long hard battle, and his mother shortly after, ovarian cancer taking her out quickly, Brad had stepped into a parental role, despite the fact that he was only a teen himself. He always looked out for his reckless kid brother, and was a real hands-on kind of guy, in the field as an explosive expert and around the house as a handyman.

Speaking of hands on...

Her gaze moved to his hands as he searched through his toolbox. He picked up a wrench, looked it over, then carefully put it back and chose another. As she thought about how meticulous he was in everything he did, her brain took a brief, luxurious moment to think about what those rough palms of his would feel like on her flesh. She imagined he was a considerate lover, and that his touches would be slow, thorough and needy, his kisses hot and demanding as he trailed a path downward, his tongue moving closer and closer to the warm juncture between her legs, to the greedy little spot that needed him the most.

"...Madison."

The sound of Brad's voice brought her thoughts crashing back to reality. She took in his watchful eyes and wondered what he'd just said to her. "Ummm," she murmured, blinking rapidly. "What was that again?"

Before Brad could answer, Jonah stepped up to her. "Are you okay?" His brows pulled into a thoughtful frown as he reached out and pressed the backs of his fingers to her forehead. "Jesus, you're burning up."

Oh God, he had no idea.

"I'm fine," she assured him and squared her shoulders. "It's just really hot in here."

She seriously needed to get it together before she threw herself at Brad and begged him to take her—right there on the wet bathroom floor. Not that Brad thought of her in a sexual way, or that she'd actually have the nerve to bare herself to him. No, that was never going to happen. Even if by some miracle Madison had the opportunity to get between the sheets with him, it was a pretty sure bet she'd run the other way, because she had a feeling Brad was the kind of guy who'd want to make love with the lights on, and take his good old time exploring his woman's body. Her skin tightened, and a strange, strangled noise caught in her throat as she imagined his attention focused on her body—his hands and eyes moving over her, touching her, seeing her. All of her.

Okay, okay, so there was no denying that she still had body image issues, and was just as insecure today as she was all those years ago. She cupped the towel against her chest tighter and darted a quick glance Brad's way.

His nostrils flared as he massaged his temples with his thumb and forefinger. "Go get changed. Now."

"Oh, right."

Adjusting the towel so it dipped in the back, making sure her backside was covered, Madison stepped past Brad and splashed her way down the hall. She could hear him digging around in his toolbox as she made a beeline to her bedroom. Once inside she shut the door and sagged against it, her libidinous body still feeling the effects of Brad's close proximity and rugged good looks. A breeze drifted in from her open window, the morning air cooling her damp body and helping to focus her thoughts.

With the gust of air giving her a burst of energy after a sleepless night, she peeled off her wet T-shirt and glanced at her clock, wondering what Brad was doing at her place so early in the morning. She tugged on her work scrubs and grabbed a clean apron from the laundry basket, then stopped dead in her tracks. Without water, she wouldn't be able to open her bakery, and if she couldn't open her doors, she'd never make enough money to find a decent place to live. Damn, damn, damn.

With so much to do today she could only hope that Brad could get the plumbing fixed right away. She took a breath to collect her thoughts, then made a mental list of everything she had to do. As soon as her assistant, and other childhood best friend, Sophie Edwards, arrived Sophie could go to work on serving the breakfast crowd—providing they had water—

while Madison darted to the country club to showcase cake samples to a bridal party. Once she got that out of the way she could get a start on making the truckload of cupcakes she'd promised to donate to the city's upcoming Fourth of July festival. The school band was counting on her donations to help raise funds for their fall trip and she didn't want to let them down.

The sound of a car pulling into the back parking lot behind the shop signaled Sophie's arrival for her shift, but if Madison couldn't open for the day, she'd have to turn her around and send her right back home. Not that she thought Sophie would mind. Working at the café and taking summer classes at night was no easy feat, and with her exams coming up, she could likely use the extra hours to study.

Smoothing her hair down and wishing the pipe had broken *after* she had showered, Madison adjusted her glasses, knotted her apron around her waist and made her way back to the brothers.

"Any luck?" she asked hopefully.

Jonah shook his head and wrung out another wet towel over the tub. "Brad doesn't have the right parts."

Her glance shot to Brad, who was down on his knees, and she swallowed hard, because from where she stood, it was abundantly clear that Brad had *all* the right parts. Then he turned his head and coughed into the crook of his arm and guilt ate at Madison.

The man was sick and the last thing he needed was to be ankle deep in icy water. This was her rental house, her mess, and she should be the one fixing it, not him.

Madison frowned. She knew what she had to do, even though she couldn't afford it. "It's okay, Brad. I'm going to call a plumber."

Brad stood and blue eyes that mirrored his brother's latched on to hers. "I can fix this for you, Madison. It's just a matter of getting the right supplies. I can do that after I drop Jonah off."

Jonah ran his hands through his short, cropped hair and looked at his watch. "Shit, I'm running late. I'll grab my gear." He cast his brother a glance. "Mind if I take a quick shower at your place before we go?"

Brad nodded and Madison stepped to the side to let her roommate push past her. With all the commotion and the brain fog from her cold, she'd forgotten that it was the first of the month and Jonah was leaving on a job this morning.

After finishing their tour in Afghanistan, both Jonah and Brad had decided to expound on their military experience and returned home to do contract bomb hunting here on American soil, defusing munitions that had been left over from former training camps during the wars. Today was Jonah's day to leave on a convoy, heading north for the next month to search for and defuse old bombs. Which, of course, accounted for why his brother had shown up at her place so early. He was here to drive Jonah to the departure site some twenty miles outside of town.

Contracting out as explosive experts was their main line of work, but when they weren't away they could be found at the old abandoned base training service dogs with their fellow comrades. With Brad's love of restoring things, he could also be found helping out in their friend's motorcycle shop, or working on the old Victorian house left to him by his ailing grandfather.

Brad tossed his gear back into his toolbox, then stood, his body crowding hers in the confided space.

When he coughed again, she said, "Brad you don't have to do this. You're not feeling well."

"Neither are you, which is why I need to get this done right away. You won't get a plumber in here for hours, and I don't want you without water for that long."

Her heart tightened at his thoughtfulness but before she could respond, she heard Sophie's voice at the foot of the stairs. "Hey, Madison, what's going on?"

"Come on up and see for yourself," Madison called out. She stepped into the hall to meet her friend, and when Sophie took one look at her hair, she crinkled her nose.

"Did you get in a fight with the egg beater?"

Great, just what she needed, her friend drawing attention to her frazzled hair. As if a red, stuffed-up nose and watery eyes weren't bad enough. Madison pulled an elastic band off her wrist and tied back her long, wet curls. "Broken pipe."

"Again?" Sophie groaned when she reached the landing.

"Yeah, because it was never fixed right in the first place," Brad's deep voice rumbled from within the bathroom.

Sophie stepped past Madison, and her eyes lit up when she spotted Brad. "Hey, Brad," she said in the same flirtatious tone she always used around the Crosby brothers. Her gaze rolled over him and Madison worked to smother a spark of jealousy she knew better than to feel. "I didn't realize you were back."

"Been back for a while now."

Surprised to hear that, Madison's head came back with a start. She hadn't seen Brad around for weeks and just assumed he was hanging out in Tallulah, Louisiana, after his friend's wedding. No doubt he'd found himself a nice, hot bridesmaid to occupy himself with.

Come to think of it, Brad had been coming around her place less and less and it made her wonder if the brothers had had a fight, although Jonah hadn't mentioned anything about it.

"So, how was the wedding?" Sophie asked.

His grin was wry, highly sardonic. "Let's just say it's good to be home." The look on his face combined with his dark tone let them both know how he felt about love and marriage. Unlike his brother, who loved to play the field and had no desire to change his lifestyle, Brad hadn't always hated the idea of settling down. In fact, he'd been engaged once himself. But it had turned out badly when he'd come back from his tour early to find his girl in bed with another guy—or at least that's what Madison had heard. He'd changed after that, dating casually, avoiding commitment, and rarely staying in one place for very long.

"Why don't you grab your stuff—" Brad gestured past Madison's shoulder, nodding toward her bedroom, "—and you can shower at my place while I drop Jonah off and make a quick trip to the hardware store."

The thought of climbing into his shower, using the same soap he'd lathered his body with earlier that morning had her nipples aching and her sex moistening. Hoping to hide her body's reaction, she coughed into her sleeve and said, "That's okay, I can just grab a shower at Sophie's."

"Only if you're really, really quiet." Sophie frowned and smoothed her blonde hair behind her ears. "Karley was up with the baby all night and the two are sleeping it off."

Madison drove her hands into her apron pockets. She'd forgotten that their friend Karley and her newborn Brooklyn were staying with Sophie until her husband returned from overseas.

"Besides," Brad said, "you don't want to spread your cold germs around."

It was true. She didn't want to risk giving her germs to an infant.

"Yeah," Sophie agreed, her expression deadpan as she nudged Madison with her elbow. "You should probably go to Brad's. That way you can make as much noise as you want. Heck, you could even scream and no one would hear you."

Fully aware of her friend's innuendo, Madison sniffed and glared at her. Oh, she was so going to kill her when she got her alone. "But then I'll be spreading my germs around his place, won't I?"

As if on cue Brad sneezed. "I've got a cold too, so it won't matter." Madison exhaled slowly, grateful that he hadn't picked up on Sophie's sexual innuendo. Giving her no time to protest, Brad slipped past them. "I'll meet you at the truck."

When he disappeared down the steps, Jonah came out from his room looking rugged and handsome dressed in his army fatigues. "Hey, Sophie," he greeted before turning to Madison. "Dibs on the first shower," he said, in typical Jonah fashion, then rushed down the steps after his brother.

A wide grin split Sophie's face as she watched him go, her gaze latched on his backside until he disappeared outside. "So," she said, "you live with one of the hottest guys I know and are about to shower at his gorgeous brother's place." Sophie tapped a painted nail on her pursed lips and Madison could almost hear the wheels turning when a sound of delight rumbled in her friend's throat. "Forget S'mores Cracker, girl-friend. I think it's high time you made yourself a *Graham Sandwich*, don't you?"

———

Jesus Christ, Madison was going to be the death of him.

He'd been hoping to avoid her when he showed up to collect his brother, and the last thing he expected was to find her in a goddamn wet T-shirt, looking so fucking hot he almost shot off a load then and there.

Brad drummed his fingers on his steering wheel and shifted in his seat, uncomfortable as his cock pressed insis-tently against his unforgiving jeans. Christ, seeing her in that T-shirt, blinking up at him with those dark bedroom eyes of hers as the lush swell of her body beckoned his touch—his cock—had damn near done him in.

Fuck.

He'd be lying if he said he didn't want her in his bed. Every time he looked at her all he could think about was caging her beneath him and fucking her long and hard, driving balls deep until she screamed out his name. Oh yeah, he'd make her scream, and when he did—contrary to what Sophie thought—*everyone* would hear it.

Maybe then he'd be able to stop thinking about her when he was alone at night. Hell, who was he kidding? He thought about her even when he wasn't alone.

He'd always liked his kid brother's best friend, but six months ago, after returning home from a long overseas tour, he suddenly began to see the sweet girl next door in different ways.

Sinful ways...

But he wasn't going to act on his urges, not when she had something going on with Jonah. Shit...

Truthfully, Brad wasn't sure what kind of relationship the two had, considering he'd seen them both date other people over the years. But from the comfort level between them, to the way they took care of each other, even going so far as to sharing a place when Jonah had finished his last tour, he knew there had to be deeper feelings involved, and he wasn't about to take her to his bed, no matter how much he wanted her naked and beneath him. Or naked and on top.

Or just plain naked.

Jonah tossed his rucksack into the truck bed and slid into the cab, pulling Brad's thoughts back from fantasyland. "Hey, bro, what's up?"

Brad put his key into the ignition and turned the engine over. "Nothing." He clenched his jaw hard as he watched Madison and Sophie exit from the downstairs bakery. A frown marred Madison's pretty face as she spoke to her friend, the

Sweetie's Bakery *Closed* sign on the door behind her rattling against the glass pane as she locked up. Brad gripped the steering wheel harder. He hated seeing her living and working in such a shitty place, and he knew today's loss of income was going to have a serious effect on her bank account.

"You have that look on your face again."

Brad angled his head toward his brother. "What look is that?"

Jonah grinned. "The one you get just before you kick the shit out of me."

Brad glared at his brother and scoffed. "Evidently, I should have beaten you more often." Okay, so he might have roughed up his punk-ass brother a time or two over the years, but it was only because Jonah had needed it. The boy was a damn fool sometimes, getting into messes that Brad had to clean up behind him.

"Yeah, well, that's a matter of opinion," Jonah said.

He held his brother's gaze. "You got something to say?"

Jonah held his hands up and laughed. "Nope."

Madison tapped on the window and Jonah jumped onto the sidewalk to let her climb into the middle. Without conscious thought Brad's eyes roamed the sexy curves she always kept hidden behind those baggy clothes and icing-stained apron. Damned if he didn't want to peel those loose-fitting work clothes from her body so he could touch and kiss her lush contours until she writhed beneath him and cried out his name.

As Madison slid in beside him, her duffle bag clutched to her chest, want pumped through his veins, the sudden, urgent need to help himself to a taste of her sweetness pulling at him hard. Fuck. He looked away, staring at some random woman walking her dog while he did his damnedest to ignore his raging hard-on.

"Here, give me that." Jonah took the bag from her and tossed it into the truck bed with his.

Once he jumped back into the cab, Brad put the vehicle into gear, turned his attention to the road ahead and slipped into traffic. Jonah punched up the volume on the radio and hooked his left arm over the back of the seat, pulling Madison toward him.

Brad tried to focus on his driving, he really did, but with Madison's leg rubbing up against his it took effort to stay on the road.

He drove through the downtown core, and when they passed a vacant building, a *For Sale* sign on the window, Jonah turned to Madison. "Maybe when I get back we can look for a new place to live."

She looked at the building, and there was a hint of gloom in her voice when she said, "I can't afford to rent an apartment *and* a business front, and it won't be easy to find a place where I can live upstairs and turn the main level into Sweetie's."

Jonah curved his arm around her and pulled her in closer. As she rested her head on his shoulder, he brushed a light kiss over her hair. "Don't worry. I'll be making some good coin out on the road. It'll go a long way in finding something nicer than we have now."

Feeling like a third wheel, an eavesdropper listening in on a private, intimate conversation, Brad cast a glance their way. His gut clenched when he saw Madison smile up at Jonah. Hell, the two of them even talked like an old married couple. There was no missing how much his brother cared for her, which only solidified Brad's vow to keep his distance where Madison was concerned.

Of course, she wasn't the first girl Brad had walked away from because of his brother. Jonah was fun, wild and had a reputation with the ladies. As teens, a few of Brad's girlfriends had gravitated toward his charismatic younger brother. Even though Brad wanted to beat the shit out of Jonah for taking his girl instead of doing the honorable thing and backing off, Brad always walked away. Blood was blood and no way would he allow a girl to come between him and his brother. How much could any of those girls have cared anyway, if they had no trouble leaving one brother for the other? Besides, he'd promised his dad that he'd take care of Jonah, and as a man of his word, he chose his family battles carefully. As long as Jonah treated the women properly, there'd be no trouble between brothers.

His thoughts careened back to a couple years ago, to the night he found his fiancée Jocelyn in bed with another man—doing the one thing he wouldn't dream of asking her to do for him, considering she'd blatantly told him oral sex was disgusting and there wasn't a girl in the world who enjoyed giving it. Although she enjoyed the hell out of it when he'd gone down on her, which he did frequently. Fuck, he wasn't sure what hurt more, seeing her mouth wrapped around some douchebag's cock, or realizing how stupid she thought he was when she starting spilling lies, telling him it wasn't what he thought. Sure, whatever. Wouldn't be the first time a woman had fallen and landed with a hard-on in her mouth and a pair of balls in her hand. Oh yeah, shit like that happened all the time.

He could have stayed and fought for her, but any girl who would sleep with another man and lie about it while her fiancé was overseas fighting for their country wasn't worth the battle. And after seeing the same thing happen to a few of his comrades, he'd come to learn that long-distance relationships never worked. Since Brad's work continued to take him out of state, he decided never to get himself in that kind of situation again. No, now he was into casual sex, no commitments.

"Besides," Jonah said, "Brad can help us turn any space into a bakery. Right, bro?"

"Yeah, sure." Brad looked at Madison, and when she turned her bright-eyed smile his way, his heart nearly stopped.

She ran paint-chipped nails along the deep hollow of her throat, and as he watched the movement his mouth watered, his tongue wanting to follow the path of her hands. Heat throbbed through him, and his cock thickened once again, aching to pound into her, hard hot strokes that would leave them both sated and breathless and would finally, *finally*, get her out of his head.

"And if something else goes wrong with the place while I'm away, Brad's your man," Jonah said.

As Brad pictured himself stepping in for his brother, his mind ran wild with one delicious idea after the other, and he forced himself to cough, hoping it would rattle some sense back into his lust-drunk brain.

"Isn't that right, Brad?"

"Yeah." He nodded. "I can help you out with anything you need."

Something flitted across her face when she asked, "Anything?"

"Yeah, anything," he assured her, but when she drew her bottom lip between her teeth, and her eyes glazed over like she had other things on her mind, he wondered if they were still talking about her run-down rental...or something else entirely.

2

Madison stepped into Brad's apartment, dropped her bag onto his scratched and pitted hardwood floor, and spread her arms wide, enjoying the coolness of the place.

"Air conditioning," she said as her eyes slipped shut. "It's heavenly."

Brad's boots scraped the floor and her lids flicked open in time to see him pick her bag up and place it on the end table next to his tattered sofa.

Jonah darted off to the shower as she exhaled slowly, her nose clearing when she breathed back in. "I think I'll stay right here for the rest of the summer."

Brad grinned. "It's fine by me, but you should know that it's only a one bedroom."

"I don't care. I'll sleep on the floor."

He drove his hands into his pockets, pulling his jeans lower on his hips, and his tone was sexy, teasing when he said, "Now what kind of guy would I be to let you sleep on the floor when I have a perfectly good bed you could use?"

Madison swallowed hard, heat curling a lazy path to her

sex as thought back to when she was a hormonal teen with a vivid imagination. She spent many nights in Brad's bed back then—without him in it. Their parents had been good friends back in the day and when her mom accompanied her dad on one of his many business trips, Brad's mom always opened her house to Madison. She'd spent many weekends there, and because Brad was usually hanging at his best friend Garrett Andersen's house, his mother used to put Madison up in his room. God, how many nights had she fantasized about him coming home unaware she was there, crawling in next to her, kissing her, touching her, making love to her all night long?

A loud noise from the street below jolted her out of her daydream. As her skin flushed hotly, she looked for a distraction. Needing a moment to compose herself, she padded across the small room to look out. Realizing Brad's place wasn't in the best of neighborhoods, she asked, "How long have you lived here?"

Brad stepped up behind her. The heat of his body engulfed her as he leaned in to look over her shoulder to see what had her attention. "Not long." His warm breath tickled the fine hairs along her neck as his raspy voice sent a barrage of erotic sensations through her body. "Just since I got back a couple months ago."

She bit back a breathy moan, her body tantalized by his closeness. She touched a crack in his window, carefully tracing the jagged pattern with her fingertip. "And you accuse me of living in a run-down place," she managed to get out as his primal essence overwhelmed her.

He gestured toward the air conditioner propped up in the open kitchen window. "Hey, at least I have air conditioning."

As she continued to trace the crack running the length of glass, he reached around and took hold of her hand. "Careful, I don't want you to cut yourself."

The work-roughened pads of his fingers scraped over her

skin, reducing her once more to that hormone-driven teen of years ago. It would be so easy to lean back, just for a minute, to see if he felt as good in real life as he did in her dreams. Instead, she stared at the crack in the glass and asked, "Do you plan to stay here long?"

His hand lingered on her wrist. "I'm not home much, so it doesn't matter where I crash. This place is as good as any when I'm not on the road." When she heard the melancholy in his voice, she turned to face him. His jaw flexed, and when she caught the intense way he was looking at her, desire singed her blood. He dipped his head, his gaze settling on her mouth, and for the briefest of moments she thought he was going to kiss her.

He inched closer, close enough for their breaths to mingle, and she wet her lips, the sweet taste of cherries dancing on her tongue. God, what would it be like to kiss him, to taste the sweetness of his mouth?

Struggling to form a coherent sentence, and looking for a distraction because she was sure she had to be misreading him—every instinct she had told her she was—she asked, "When do you go back on the road again?"

"At the end of the month."

"After Jonah returns?" she asked.

At the mention of his brother, his nostrils flared and he jerked back like a grenade had just gone off. "Yeah," he said, his tone harder. "When Jonah returns." There was a moment of tense silence as he hovered close, then he spun around and walked away from her. "I...uh...I have to get some supplies from storage."

As she watched him stalk to his door and slam it behind him, she once again wondered if the brothers had had a fight. She stepped away from the window and walked around his sparse apartment, thinking how desolate the place looked. It occurred to her that Jonah traveled just as much as Brad, but he at least added some personal touches to the bedroom he rented from her. Brad didn't just live like a bachelor, he lived like a nomad. With no commitments or attachments, he was ready to pick up and leave at a moment's notice.

Madison gave a sad shake of her head, understanding his ex-fiancée had done one hell of a number on him. Too bad really, because Brad was a great guy who deserved a house full of kids and happily ever after, considering there was a time when he wanted that. And she couldn't forget he had that big old Victorian house just waiting for him, yet he preferred to live in a one-bedroom rental. Madison's heart grew heavy. What would it take for him to get over his ex's betrayal and move on? Of course, for all she knew, he could be pining for Jocelyn, hoping she'd come back to him.

Brad returned, clutching what looked like a welding torch, just as Jonah stepped from the steamy bathroom.

Jonah raked his hand through his wet hair, tossed his bag over his shoulder and gave Madison one last look before he made his way to the door. "Are you sure you're feeling okay? You still look flushed."

She stifled a yawn, exhaustion from the cold once again pulling at her. "I just need a shower," she assured him.

He pointed toward the bedroom. "And maybe a nap."

At the mention of Brad's bed and his offer to share it with her, need gathered in the pit of her stomach and her sex clenched with want.

Once again a strange noise crawled out of her throat and Jonah eyed her with uncertainty before he slapped his brother on the back. "Promise me you'll take care of her while I'm gone?"

Brad turned, averting his brother's gaze. "Yeah, sure. I promise." Then he looked at Madison just as a sneeze wracked her body. Something in his face softened when he said, "I'll lock up on my way out. There are clean towels in the closet. Go get a shower. You know where the bedroom is if you want to lie down. I'll be back after I get your plumbing fixed."

She glanced at the clock. "I have an eleven o'clock appointment at the country club. I have cake samples made back at the bakery and need to bring them to the bridal party."

Brad gave an understanding nod. "Okay, then. I'll come back and get you before I head to your place."

Madison watched them go and after she heard the lock click into place, she walked into the steamy bathroom. She stripped off her clothes and folded them neatly, then wiped the mirror, hardly able to believe one of her fantasies was about to come true. Of course, in her fantasies, when she climbed into Brad's shower, he was always in there with her.

She turned on the hot spray and stepped into the stall. After locating a bar of soap on the ledge, she picked it up and ran it over her body. Her eyes drifted shut, imagining it was Brad's hands on her, slicking over her breasts and toying with her hard nipples. She ran the soap lower, until it was between her quivering legs. She brushed it over her engorged clit and shivered, her skin tingling all over as she indulged in her erotic fantasy for an extra moment.

When the water started to turn cold, she yelped, quickly rinsed off and climbed out. She searched her bag for deodorant. "Shoot," she mumbled, then glanced at Brad's medicine cabinet.

She did a quick shoulder check, even though she knew she was alone in the bathroom, but couldn't help feeling like she was invading his privacy as she inched open the mirror. She peeked inside, and her knees weakened when she found a box of condoms. Madison gulped and picked up the box. It gave her an odd sense of satisfaction to find it unopened. It was silly really. Of course Brad had sex. Hell, so did she! Well, not recently, but still...

She put the box back and nosed around in his cabinet a bit more. She gave a small spray of his cologne, then grabbed his stick of deodorant. She uncapped it and drew in the scent. *Brad...* She applied it to her underarms, recapped it and put it back in his cabinet. Making sure she had everything back in its place, Madison closed the mirror and dressed for her eleven o'clock meeting. Turning her attention to her tangled hair, she took out her blow dryer and flat iron. Once she fought her wayward curls into submission, she slipped in her contacts, presenting Made-Up Madison to the world, instead of "Fatty Maddy".

Even though she was more comfortable dressed in her loose-fitting clothes and glasses, with her hair tied back in a ponytail, she reserved that look for home, or for when she was elbow deep in pastry dough at the back of the bakery. When she was out on deliveries or showcasing her product to potential clients, she presented a different side of herself, even though she wasn't all that comfortable in form-fitting clothes. But she was a businesswoman and had to present herself as one, which meant sweats were out.

Feeling more like her old self after showering and dressing, she padded around Brad's small apartment. She stepped over his laundry basket of clean, neatly folded clothes, honing in on a pair of boxer briefs lying on top of the pile. She resisted the urge to pick them up. With the way her day was going, Brad would likely catch her in the act, or worse, think she was some kind of underwear perv. Instead she gifted herself with a moment to visualize him in them and nothing else, and as a warm whisper curled around her thighs, she plopped down on the sofa, where she grabbed her phone from her purse in search of a distraction. As she scrolled through emails, she heard the key in the lock.

Nervous anticipation welled up inside her and she worked to tamp it down. Good God, she'd known Brad her entire life, and it was damn well time she stopped acting like a love-struck schoolgirl around him. She took a centering breath and squared her shoulders.

"Hey," he said. Despite the fact that she'd just lectured herself on keeping her cool around him, the second she set eyes on him her knees went weak.

She climbed from the sofa, walked around his laundry basket and tried for normal. "Were you able to get the parts?"

"Yeah," he answered, then he angled his head, his eyes clouding with something that resembled desire as his gaze trailed the length of her body. His throat worked as he swallowed and, if she wasn't mistaken, she thought she spotted hunger in his baby blues as he looked at her form-fitting dress clothes. But she had to be mistaken. Brad had never looked at her as anything more than his kid brother's friend. Then again, she'd only started wearing professional outfits after opening her bakery last year, which meant that until today, until this very moment, he'd never seen her dressed in anything but unflattering sweats that hid her body before. Had never seen her dress like one of the put-together, brazen women he'd normally go for. And from the way he was currently staring at her, interesting flickering in the back of his eyes, it seemed like he was actually noticing her.

Still, she had to be mistaken, right?

Laid out on his side on Madison's wet, tiled bathroom floor, Brad finished cutting the wall away to give him better access to the pipes, but how he was supposed to concentrate with Madison prancing around in those high heels of hers was beyond him.

She stopped by the bathroom door for the umpteenth time. "You sure you don't need anything before I go?"

Oh, he needed something all right.

"I'm good."

She pointed to her medicine cabinet and he watched the way her blouse tightened on her breasts. "I just have to brush my teeth, then I'll be out of your way."

"Yeah, okay," he managed around a tongue gone thick. She went up on her toes, and he shifted restlessly at the sight of her curvy ass in that tight pencil skirt, her high heels giving her lush cheeks a sexy lift.

"Fuck," he murmured under his breath as he assessed the pipes.

"What?"

"Nothing. There's just some water still leaking so I have to drain the system."

"Oh, did you want me to do that for you?"

"Not dressed like that I don't."

An almost uncomfortable look came over her face as she gave herself a once over. "My meeting—" she started to explain, but he climbed to his feet and cut her off.

"I've got it," he said, his cock needing a reprieve from the sexy yet professional clothes draping her body before he did permanent damage to himself. Honestly, it didn't matter what she wore. Even dressed in sweats she rubbed him the wrong way, or the right way...or...fuck...if only she'd rub him.

He took the stairs two at a time until he reached the basement. He found the water tank and went to work on draining the system. Once complete he hurried back upstairs. He stepped back into the bathroom, and his feet splashed on the water still pooling on the tile. The hurried sound of Madison's high heels clicking on the stairs behind him had him spinning around.

Her voice sounded rushed when she rounded the corner and said, "Oh, I forgot to tell you... Whoa!"

She hurried into the bathroom so fast, her body crashed with his. His feet slipped on the floor, and he tried to grab on to something to right himself, but the impact had him faltering backward.

"Shit," he yelled, knowing he was going down for the count and there wasn't a damn thing he could do about it.

His boots went out from underneath him and he fell backward with an undignified oomph, Madison crashing to the floor right along with him.

His head connected with something unforgiving on the way down, but he couldn't concentrate on the pain shooting down his arm, not when Madison's floral hair fell over his face in a tumbled mess, and her soft body landed on top of his in the most erotic ways.

"Sorry," she squeaked out. "I didn't expect you to be standing there."

His hands slipped around her waist and settled on the small of her back. He sucked in a breath. "What...uh...what was it you forgot to tell me?" he asked.

She pushed her hair off her face, her mouth only inches from his. "Oh, I just wanted to let you know I made you a sandwich in case you got hungry. It's in the pastry fridge."

Her lush warm body felt so good on top of his...so fucking good...his cock grew an inch. She squirmed, like she was about to slide off, but he held her tight.

He pinned her to him and groaned. "Stop squirming."

"Why?" she asked, her voice sounding breathless.

"Because you don't want to get wet."

Her eyes widened and her lips inched open. "Wet?" she asked, her breathing becoming a little harsher, more erratic. "Why...why would I get wet?" Everything in the way she said wet sounded so sinful, and he couldn't help but wonder how wet he could make her, if given the chance.

He jerked his head to the side. "The floor. It's still wet. If you slide off, you'll get your clothes wet. You won't be able to go to your meeting if your clothes are all wet."

Christ, how many times could he say wet in one sentence?

"Right. Right. I knew that was what you meant." She frowned. "How am I supposed to get up?"

"Hold on to me."

With her body molded to his, he wrapped one arm around her waist while he pushed himself up off the floor with the other. She snaked her arms around his shoulders and held tight as he climbed to his feet.

Once upright, his head began spinning. Feeling dizzy, the room tumbling out of control around him, he stumbled, slamming her against the wall as he tried to regain his balance. Shit, maybe he'd hit his head harder than he first thought.

Madison gasped, and when her sweet, minty breath wafted before his nostrils all coherent thought fled. Her lush body fit so perfectly next to his, and her soft breasts were so hot against his chest that all he could think about was kissing her, having his way with her right here against the wall. Christ, what could one little taste hurt? One tiny fucking nibble...

As the bathroom faded in and out of existence, her voice sounded as if it were thousand miles away. He pushed against her, caging her with his body. Knowing he wasn't thinking straight, he dipped his head, and even though she was speaking, saying something to him, he couldn't hear her, not when his entire focus was on that sweet mouth of hers.

Before he could get his shit together, he closed his mouth over hers, and when he heard a heated groan, he wasn't sure whether it was his or hers. He sank into her mouth, reveling in the delicious taste of her. With little finesse, he pushed his tongue inside to play with hers. *So fucking sweet*. Greed urged him on and his tongue slashed against her mouth, his cock aching to sink inside her wet heat and stay there for the rest of the day. Jesus, her mouth tasted like mint, cherry and sugar all rolled into one—the best thing he'd ever tasted.

Some part of his brain registered that her hands were on his body, touching, tugging at his shirt, pulling on his shoulders. Jesus, did this mean she wanted him as much as he wanted her? But when she raked her fingers through his hair and pain zinged through him, reality crashed over him like the cold water from her broken pipe.

He inched back and stared at her. When he saw the way he'd smudged her lipstick and mussed her hair, and noted the almost frightened look in her eyes, his heart raced. Okay, so apparently her hands were all over him because she was trying to push him away, not because she was eager to touch him. What the fuck was he thinking?

"Jesus, Madison. I didn't mean—"

"Brad." She carefully smoothed her hand over the back of his head. "I think you have a concussion."

His hand went to this head, and when her fingers moved aside he found an egg-sized lump and winced. "Shit."

"You must have hit your head when you fell."

"Yeah, I...uh." His glance went to her mouth again. "I'm sorry."

"Don't be sorry. You're just not in your right frame of mind right now. I don't think you even knew what you were doing."

Oh, he knew all right.

"You need to sit," she said, her beautiful breasts rising and falling as she stared at him, wide-eyed.

"I'm fine," he murmured, inching back.

"You're not fine. Come with me." She grabbed his hand and took him to her bedroom. She sat and patted the mattress beside her. "I think I'd better cancel my eleven o'clock."

In a bid to appease her, Brad dropped down next to her on the bed. "You're not canceling anything."

"You shouldn't be alone."

"Madison, I'm fine." She frowned and he suspected there was only one way to get her to leave. He pushed his index finger into her sheets. "If I promise to stay here until you get back, will you go?"

She rolled her eyes. "Yeah, Brad. I was just born yesterday."

He grinned. "You know me too well."

"What I know is how stubborn you are." She tugged at his T-shirt. "At least get out of these wet clothes."

There was that word *wet* again. He shouldn't tease her, but he couldn't seem to stop himself from responding with, "So what you're saying is you want me naked and in your bed."

Her dark eyes widened and she opened her mouth and closed it again. "I just don't want... You have a cold..."

"Fine. If I grab something of Jonah's to wear and promise to take it easy, will you go?"

She glanced at her clock and climbed from the bed. "Okay, but I'm getting you ice first and if you need me, call my cell."

Twenty minutes later, Brad listened to the sound of her car leaving the driveway. He dropped the ice-filled cloth into her bathroom sink and checked the copper pipes to see if they were dry enough to solder.

Satisfied that they were, he grabbed his gear from his toolbox and lost track of time as he went to work on fixing her faulty plumbing. Before he knew it the afternoon was upon them and Madison was back from her appointment. Her heels clicked on the stairs as she came to check on him.

"Brad," she called out as she cautiously turned the corner, walking slowly like she was trying to avoid another run-in with him. And who could blame her, considering how he'd ravished her, damn near taking what wasn't his to take.

Sitting on the edge of her tub, Brad turned off his soldering gun, and said, "I'm here."

She stepped into the bathroom and looked at the gaping hole in her wall. She crinkled her nose when her glance went back to him. "You didn't change your clothes."

He shrugged. "They were only going to get wet anyway."

For a moment she looked like she was going to give him a lecture, but then she looked beyond his shoulders and asked, "How's it going?"

"Almost done. You'll have running water in no time at all. Then I'll see about fixing this wall."

She shook her head. "You've done enough already. And don't think I forgot about that bang to the head."

He ignored her protest. "How did you make out at the country club?"

She smiled. "I got the contract. Which means I really need to get to work."

"Almost there," he assured her. "I'll give you a shout when I'm done."

"I'll leave you to it then." She clicked her way down the hall, his focus locked on her curvy ass the whole way. When she reached her bedroom, he shifted his position for a better view and damn near swallowed his tongue when she kicked off her heels and tore off her blouse, clearly forgetting that he had direct line of sight from the bathroom. She probably never expected him to be sneaking a peak. After all, they'd been friends for years and she was dating his brother.

A gorgeous lace bra covered her ample breasts, and his gaze latched on to the creamiest cleavage he'd ever had the pleasure of viewing. His cock tightened and his nostrils flared, heat careening through his blood at dangerous speeds. He wet his mouth as the need to taste her set his body on fire. He was so goddamn hot, burning from the inside out, he was sure he could smell smoke. He inhaled then jerked back with a start.

Wait! He *could* smell smoke.

He jumped from the tub. "Fuck."

"Brad," Madison called out, rushing down the hall. She tied the waistband on her sweats. "I smell smoke."

"Me too." He pushed past her and rushed down the stairs to the basement, Madison tight on his heels. He reached her furnace room and cursed under his breath when he saw her water tank smoking. His glance went to her circuit board, and he raked his hands through his hair, kicking his ass for forgetting. But goddammit, he wasn't in his right mind when he was around Madison.

"Shit."

"What happened?" Madison asked.

"I drained the tank but forgot to switch the breaker. I burnt out the heating element." He walked to the circuit board and flicked off the breaker. "I'll have to run out and get a new one. Water might be coming a little later than I had hoped." He drove his hands into his pockets and shook his head. Jesus, he'd told her not to call a plumber because he could fix it for her, and what a fine mess he was making of that. "I'm sorry, Madison."

She touched his shoulder. "Hey, don't be sorry. I just appreciate what you're doing for me."

With the heat of her hand seeping into his wet flesh, he could feel his body reacting, hardening. Need careened through him and his glance dropped to her mouth. For the briefest of moments he thought about kissing her again, but doubted he could get away with blaming it on his concussion a second time. She was too smart for that, and if she knew how much he wanted her it would make things awkward between the three of them when Jonah returned.

"I have some paperwork to take care of anyway, so going without water for a little longer won't hurt me."

He took note of the tank's model number. "I'll be back as fast as I can."

Brad climbed into his truck and spent the next few hours driving around town. Her tank was old and getting the right part proved harder than he expected. When he finally arrived back at her place, night was upon them and his stomach was growling, not to mention the throbbing at the base of his neck. Shit, maybe he really should have taken it easy.

He parked in the small parking lot and fished out the key Jonah had given him from his pocket. But when he found Madison standing at the bakery door, waving him over, he secured the new heating element under his arm and walked toward her.

Her eyes narrowed as they moved over his face in concern. "Everything okay?"

"Yeah, it just took longer than I thought."

"Come on."

She led him inside the dimly lit bakery that always smelled like sweet icing sugar, like Madison herself. Then another scent caught him. Pizza.

"Have a seat and eat with me." Madison pointed to one of the many tables scattered throughout the small space.

He held up the heating element. "Let me get this done first."

His stomach took that moment to grumble, and Madison took the part from him. "You've done enough for today. Time to eat."

Hunger pangs gnawed at him. "Yeah, that does sound like a good idea." He grabbed a chair and Madison divvyed up the pizza before handing him a cola.

"It might be a little bit cold. I was waiting for you."

He felt a strange hitch in his chest. "You waited for me?"

She nodded, then looked at the dim lights. "I have to keep them low, otherwise customers might think I'm open."

He grinned. "The *Closed* sign hanging on the door doesn't do the trick."

She laughed. "Apparently not. Customers still come up to the door and peek into the window. But I guess I'm grateful that customers like my goods enough they they'll stop by at all hours."

Her customers weren't the only ones, he thought, as his glance moved over *her* goods. Oh yeah, he liked them enough that he'd stop by at all hours too.

She continued to talk about her business, and how she'd like to hire more staff to keep later hours. He listened to her ideas and scarfed down his first piece in record time, following each bite with a swig of his cola.

"Have some more." Madison nudged the box toward him.

He helped himself to more and as he chewed he noticed sauce on Madison's face. He grabbed a napkin, and without giving it another thought, swiped at it, but when his fingers connected with her soft flesh, something that looked an awful lot like heat moved across her face.

"You…uh…you have sauce on your face," he explained and jerked his hand back. As the air charged and his blood ran south, he quickly changed the subject. "I guess it's going to be hard for you with Jonah away for a month."

He watched her throat work as she swallowed and realized it felt a little odd sitting in the dark bakery with her like this, a little intimate. "I kind of got used to the company, and because I don't have an alarm system, I sleep better when he's here."

"He takes good care of you?"

"Yeah, Jonah might be a lot of things," she said, a knowing grin on her face, "but he's good to me."

"That's good." Brad stuffed his face before he said something he might regret, like how she should ditch his punk-ass brother and give him a chance. But he'd never do that to Jonah, no matter how much he wanted Madison for himself.

Madison finished eating and said, "Wait here, I'll be right back."

Brad pushed back in his chair and looked around her bakery as she disappeared into the kitchen area. He was impressed that she'd built the business from the ground up and was garnering quite the loyal following in town and in the wedding circuits. Too bad she had to start out in such a crappy building, and if he ever came face to face with her landlord, he was going to give him a good shit kicking.

Madison stepped up behind him, ice clinking in a bag.

"What are you doing?" he asked.

He was about to turn but her hand on his shoulder stopped him. "Shh, just let me check your head, okay?"

Her body crowded his as she carefully placed the ice on his lump. How long had it been since someone had taken care of him? Not since before his mother had passed. That Madison was the one caring for him now caused a tightening in his gut.

"It's still very swollen," she said quietly.

Oh, she seriously had no idea.

"Did you ice it earlier when I told you to?"

He shifted, ready to grab the bag and place it on a different body part.

"Yeah," he mumbled. "Sort of."

She huffed. "You really need to take better care of yourself."

He made a move to get up, this nurturing side of her making him feel all peculiar inside, making him remember his own upbringing and the way his mother showered her boys with love before cancer took her shortly after his father's heart attack. Their love was so strong that Brad couldn't help but think her death came on the heels of his father's quickly because it was nature's way of putting husband and wife back together again.

His heart tightened with memories of his folks and his happy childhood. Brad had always wanted a family of his own, and just when he thought it was within reach, his ex had betrayed him, and ever since his world had been tilted off balance.

He cleared his throat, unease moving through him. "Let me get at the tank, okay?"

With the bag still on his head, she shifted, and perched on the table beside him. She yawned, and said quietly, "Let's leave it for tonight."

"No. I'm not leaving you here without water."

"I'll be fine."

He gave her a crooked grin. "Now look who's being stubborn."

"You've done enough." Warm brown eyes full of genuine concern moved over his face. "Besides you're fighting a cold and I think you have a concussion."

He exhaled slowly, exhaustion moving through his body now that he stopped working. "Okay, how about this. I'll call it a night if you agree to stay at my place."

Her body tightened and she opened her mouth to say something when he cut her off. "I'm not leaving you without water. So either I fix this tonight, or you stay at my place."

"I don't think—"

"Besides, I have a concussion," he said, wincing with a little too much enthusiasm as he took the bag of ice from her. "And I don't think I'm supposed to be alone."

She chuckled quietly and shook her head. "You always did know how to get what you wanted didn't you?"

Not always...

He arched a brow. "So...?"

"Fine." She pushed off the table.

He grabbed her arm and softened his voice when he added, "It's what Jonah would have wanted me to do."

Her eyed dimmed as she looked at some distant spot past his shoulder, letting him know how much she adored his brother. His gut clenched wishing she'd look at him like that.

"Okay, I'll sleep on the sofa," she said quietly.

He nodded, even though he had no intention of letting her crash on his couch, but now was not the time to be arguing about such things.

"Just let me grab my stuff."

As soon as she left he pulled his cell from his pocket and made a call. He spoke quietly as Madison made her way upstairs, and just as he was about to hang up, he heard Madison behind him.

"Brad, do you want—" Her voice fell off when she saw the phone in his hand. "Oh, I'm sorry. If I'm keeping you from someone..."

He shut down his phone, shoved it in his pocket, and shook his head. "That was Granddad. I normally visit him on Wednesdays and bring one of the therapy dogs by but I don't want to go around the nursing home with a cold."

The alarm fell from her face and a smile touched her mouth as she looked at him. "Oh, I thought." She shook her head. "Never mind."

"What were you asking me?"

She held out a blister pack. "Cold medication. It's supposed shorten the duration of a cold, but it also knocks you right out." She yawned, then laughed. "I took one upstairs and bed is already calling me."

He took her duffle bag from her and put the cold medication in his pocket. "Well, then let me get you to bed." He suddenly wondered if he was some kind of masochist. Christ, he should have just fixed her tank, because he had no idea how he was going to make it through the night with her in his bed and his hands tied.

Hands tied...

Ah, fuck.

3

A mosaic of stars lit up the night as they made their way back to Brad's place. He stole a glance at Madison in the passenger seat and could see her lids slipping shut, only to spring back open again like she was trying to stay awake. The combination of medication and wear on her body from the cold were obviously getting the better of her.

"Hey," he said quietly, the streetlight falling over them. "Just close your eyes and sleep. I'll wake you when we get there."

She nodded and whispered, "I'm okay."

"You're not okay. Whatever you took is knocking you out."

"Yeah." Her voice was drowsy and soft. "I know." She bit her lip and looked out the window as he took the corner, his apartment building not too far off now. Her voice was low, barely audible when she said, "Are you sure I'm not putting you out?"

"Close your eyes, Madison."

She exhaled slowly and leaned her head back on the seat.

A short while later, when he pulled up in front of his building and killed the ignition, she rolled her head on the seat and blinked heavy lids at him.

"Let's go." He pulled the keys. "You can have the bed."

Stubbornness moved over her face. "I'm not going to sleep in your bed."

"Don't worry, I'm not going to be in it," he said, and then in an attempt to keep things light, when all he wanted to do was strip her naked and have his way with her, he added, "Besides, I'm pretty sure that's not what Jonah meant when he asked me to take care of you for him." He stiffened at the mention of Jonah, and she opened her mouth to say something when he cut her off. "And it's not like you haven't slept in my bed before."

"What are you talking about?"

"Years ago, when you used to stay at the house. Mom always gave you my bed."

"How did you know that?"

He breathed deep, catching hints of her sweet aroma. "Because no matter how many times the sheets were washed, I could still smell you on them."

"You could...smell me?"

"Yeah, your scent was all over my room."

She crinkled her nose. "My...my scent. What scent?"

"Cherry." He worked to swallow the moan crawling out of his throat. "You always smelled like cherry. Still do."

She wet her lips and his eyes dropped to her mouth, his cock aching so hard all he could think about doing was pulling her under him and taking her right there in the cab of the truck. "It's my—"

"I know what it is." He shifted closer, need urging him to answer the demands of his body.

A car horn hocked, the shrill sound knocking some sense back into him. He pulled back and exhaled slowly. "Let's go."

They climbed from the truck and he grabbed her bag. Keeping her close as they walked across the dark parking lot, he led her inside the building and up the stairs to his apartment. Once inside, she looked around hesitantly, like she didn't know what to do next. It made him want to draw her close, to reassure her that everything was okay as he stripped off her clothes to show her just how right things could be between them.

She doesn't belong to you, dude.

He handed over her duffle bag and she gave him a look that conveyed her uncertainty.

"The bedroom is that way." He pointed down the hall, dismissing her. "G'night."

"Oh," she said, and something that looked like surprise and disappointment flashed in her eyes. "Okay." She pulled her bag closer to her chest and took a step toward the hall. He watched her and wanted to kick himself for being an ass. By rights he should make her something warm to drink, run her a hot bath, or at least see if she needed a glass of water on her nightstand. But Jesus, he needed her away from him before he threw caution to the wind, forgot she was his brother's girl, and drew her in for a real kiss, one he wouldn't apologize for this time.

His cock tightened as his lips twitched. "G,night," he said again under his breath, a headache brewing.

"Okay. G'night." She stopped and turned back to him. "Brad?"

"Yeah?"

"Thank you."

His heart squeezed inside his chest. Christ, she was so fucking sweet. Here he was giving her the brush off, acting cold and indifferent because he needed her as far away from him as possible, and despite all that she was thanking him. Fuck, where was Garrett when he needed him? His best friend would have no problem giving Brad an ass kicking to help him get his head on straight. He grabbed his cell, needing to get out for a beer, but then quickly powered it down. He'd have to get used to the idea that Garrett was no longer a bachelor, ready to hit the bar at a moment's notice. Now that he was with Tallulah, and they had a baby on the way, he had other commitments and the last thing he needed tonight was to hear Brad whining to him about Madison.

Once she disappeared inside his room, Brad darted to the bathroom, needing a cold shower and something to occupy his mind, because if he for one minute thought about her sprawled across his bed, he might not be able to stop himself from going in there.

After showering, he reached into his pants pockets to empty them before tossing them into the laundry. He found Madison's cold medication. Hell, maybe he should take one or two. At least if he was flat out on his back, dead to the world on the couch, he wouldn't have to fight the temptation to ravish her.

He grabbed a pair of clean boxer briefs from the laundry basket in his living room, and after pulling them on, pushed a couple pills through the blister pack. Needing something to wash them down with, he grabbed a beer from the fridge. Yeah, mixing the two probably wasn't his best move, but goddammit he wanted the combination to knock the shit right out of him.

He grabbed a blanket and pillow from the small linen closet and threw himself down on the couch. He flicked on the TV, hoping the sound would drown out the world around him. Soon enough cars on the road below became a distant buzz as his body shut down for the night.

His mind drifted, and a long time later he woke to the glow of the television. He swallowed the dryness in his throat and reached for the remote. Still half-asleep, he flicked the television off and made his way to the kitchen for a drink of water. He stood before the air conditioner letting it cool his body before he put his mouth under the tap. He took a long swallow, then made his way to his bed, his body craving a few more hours sleep.

He climbed into his side but there was something niggling at his brain, something he was supposed to remember. Except at the moment he was too damn tired to care, the medication and concussion pulling him under like a tsunami wave. Whatever it was, he'd figure it out in the morning.

He drifted off to sleep, but he slept restlessly, his mind dreaming of Madison. Dreaming of kissing her, stripping away those sweats she wore to expose her lush body, and making her cry out his name as he made her come for him. Jesus, the things he'd do to make her come...if only she were his.

With his body hot and needy he rolled to his side to find the object of his dreams beside him, her long hair sprawled across the pillow. He growled low in his throat, his cock throbbing for him to take her. A riot of emotions overcame him and he cursed, knowing he had to still be dreaming, because there was no way Madison would be in his bed with him.

"Fuck," he murmured under his breath.

He closed his eyes, his cock throbbing, begging for release, but when he opened them again she was still there. He shifted closer and even in his semi-sleep state he could smell cherry, and something else, something that smelled like him. Christ, he really had to be sleeping because no way would *his* scent be all over her, not when he hadn't put it there. He filled his lungs with her aroma and his body came alive, prickling with want as she saturated his sheet with her perfumed skin.

She angled her head to the side, exposing the long, silky

column of her neck. A groan crawled out of his throat as his mind shifted through all the things he wanted to do to her. He reached out and ran his finger along the sexy length of her throat, his raging hard-on pushing through his boxers—demanding attention.

His touch roused her, and she blinked. With her lids barely open, and her eyes hardly focused she groggily asked, "Is this a dream?"

"Yeah, baby. This is a dream."

She stretched out and he moved closer, running his hands along her soft, voluptuous curves. He dragged his fingers over her thighs until he reached the hem of her nightshirt. He gripped it and pushed it up to expose her body. When he glimpsed her bare pussy, he shook from head to toe, knowing for sure this was a dream, because in his fantasy world, Madison never wore panties. Ever.

He closed his palm over one breast, and squeezed, kneading her flesh between his fingers like it was pliable dough. She writhed and placed one hand over his while the other went to her bare breasts, to give it the attention it craved. She plucked her nipple, and as he watched the pale pink bud stiffen he damn near sobbed with pleasure.

"So good," she murmured, and he didn't miss the raw ache of lust in her voice.

Brad licked his parched lips, pleasure forking through him. Jesus, her body was hot, so fucking hot for him. He climbed on top of her, pinning her beneath him as he buried his face in her neck. He caressed the long hollow of her throat with his lips, then lifted his head and practically howled as he reveled in the candied taste of her skin. He licked her flesh, trailing lower until he reached her full breasts. He drew an engorged nipple into his mouth and sucked as his hands crushed her hair. Unable to get enough of her in his mouth, he nibbled and bit, until their moans mingled.

He shifted slightly and reached between her legs to find her pussy hot, ready, her curls damp with passion. Sweet mother of God! Hunger driving him, he forcefully pushed open her legs, barreling his way in. He knew he was being rough, overly demanding, but this was his dream, goddammit, and he'd wanted her for so fucking long now there was nothing he could do to slow himself down.

Without waiting for an invitation, he inserted a finger into her slick folds. So soft. So goddamn fucking soft. He swirled his finger in her heat and he salivated as she bucked against him. The need to taste her had his body shaking, his blood burning hot.

Pressure built inside him and his heart rate doubled as he slid down her body. Carnal desire swept over him. He pulled in air yet couldn't seem to fill his lungs. His cock throbbed, a red-hot rod desperate to drive inside her tight, fluttering walls. Desperate to fuck the hell right out of her, he grabbed her legs and spread them impossibly wider, then shoved his face between her thighs. She made a noise—a hot, sexy bedroom sound—as she ground her honeyed pussy against his mouth. He found her clit and pulled it between his teeth. His body spasmed, pre-come dripping from his slit as the need to taste her cream, to have her to come on his face, in his mouth, drove him on.

He pushed another finger inside her and she clawed at the sheets. Her hips came off the bed, her pussy growing slicker with each stroke. His head began reeling, his entire being intoxicated by her taste, the erotic sight of her naked body trapped beneath him.

He pumped harder, his mouth pressing hungrily. He swiped his tongue over her clit, pushing her closer and closer to the precipice, but never allowing her to tumble over.

Lacking any sort of inhibition, she ground against his face, writhing and moaning and taking what she needed.

"Please," she begged, her pretty pink tongue snaking out to dampen her lips.

At the frustration, the need he heard in her voice, he decided to give her what her body was craving. He switched tactics and amped up the pressure, and a second later he could feel her desire mounting, her body reaching the point of no return.

"Oh God," she cried out, her walls clenching hard around his fingers as she gave herself over to the pleasure.

His dry throat cracked but as she came for him, he quickly rehydrated himself with her cream, licking and savoring every last drop. As her sweet taste teased his senses, hunger consumed him, and the need to fuck her and fuck her hard, was the only thought clanging around in his lust-rattled head. He tore off his briefs and climbed back up her body. He buried his face in her neck and in one quick thrust he entered her, pushing himself in balls deep.

Sweet fuck!

As her heat closed around him—torturing the living hell out of him—he moved urgently over her body, unable to slow himself down, unable to assuage the need inside him. His blood rushed, every sensation so intense. So fucking intense.

Less than a gentleman in this dream, he fucked her like a goddamn rutting animal. Her nails scraped his back and his body burned hot, pleasure like he'd never before experienced swamping him. His brain buzzed and his cock throbbed, but he didn't want to come just yet. Not just yet.

She moaned as he pulled his rock hard cock all the way out of her hot pussy and slid off the mattress. Far from done with her, he grabbed her ankles and her groan of displeasure turned into a moan of pleasure as he flipped her over. He shoved a pillow underneath her hip, raising her curvaceous ass in the air.

Ah Jesus...

She was perfect. So fucking perfect.

The sexy silhouette of her body waiting for his cock, her hot little ass begging for a spanking, had his muscles bunching. He climbed back onto the bed and grunted as he impaled her with one hard thrust. She clawed at the sheets, her tight muscles clenching, the erotic pulse a sure sign that she was coming for him again. Longing ripped through him as her liquid desire dripped over his shaft and trickled down his leg in mind fucking ways.

His body shook violently. Heat blasted through him, and he felt like he was caught in a grenade fire as sparks exploded before his eyes and rocked the ground beneath him.

Christ, this might not be real but never had he felt so alive. Lacking any sort of gentleness, he roughly ran unsteady hands over her ass, his adrenaline spiking as he grunted and rode her with abandonment. Her pussy muscles gripped his dick as he rammed her, the pressure brewing between his legs damn near rendering him senseless.

As he floated on some level between sleep and awake, he knew this was the hottest, craziest fucking sex he'd ever had, and nothing...nothing...in reality had ever felt this good.

He slammed with such a force he was sure they were going to break the bed, but he needed, oh Christ how he needed. His breath came in ragged bursts, and his whole body trembled. Never had he felt so crazed, frantic with the need to fuck. He bit the inside of his cheek and fought the urge to come, never wanting this moment to end, but the need to release became so intense it was almost painful. He trembled from head to toe, and concentrated on the sensations as her aromas fueled his lust.

Burning up, he pulled his cock out, and then jerked his

hips forward, driving every inch back inside her tight sheath. A wheezing sound crawled out of his throat and his brains shut down, nothing existing but this moment, this woman. Christ he was lost, so damn lost in her. She squeezed her pussy muscles around his dick, and he knew he was fighting a losing battle, his restraint a thing of the past.

"Ah fuck," he grunted, his balls tightening as he shuddered in surrender. His nostrils flared and his jaw clenched as an orgasm exploded through him. With his fingers biting into her hips, bruising her skin, he splashed his seed inside her, wanting nothing more than to leave them both a hot, wet mess when this was over.

He stayed on top of her for a long time, until his cock stopped pulsing and her body went limp. By small degrees he pulled out, and she whimpered when he slid off her and sprawled out beside her. She rolled over onto her back and he pulled her close. When she rested her head on his shoulder and released a contented sigh, he felt a small measure of panic, suddenly unnerved by how real this all felt.

4

Bright rays of light slanting on the bedroom wall pulled Madison awake. She stretched and breathed deep, happy that her nose was clear and the medication seemed to have kicked her cold to the curb. Blinking her eyes open, she shot a glance around the room, her fuzzy mind trying to figure out where she was as her joints groaned in protest. She shifted, and when muscles that she hadn't used in far too long ached in the most delightful ways, she jackknifed upright and shot a glance from left to right.

"Oh my God!" she said when she found Brad sprawled out beside her, his gorgeous body completely uncovered, completely naked, and calling out to her in the most sinful ways. She bit her bottom lip and her fingers twitched as memories of last night—her dream—crashed over her.

Except, she quickly realized, it hadn't been a dream at all. She'd had sex with Brad.

She'd had sex with Brad!

But not only did she have sex—unbelievable, orgasmic, mind-blowing sex—with him, she acted like a goddamn wanton woman. Lacking any sort of inhibition, she'd ground her pussy against his face, moaning and groaning without censure, and even going so far to touch herself in front of him. Oh Christ, in her drug-induced semi-conscious state, she did lascivious, down and dirty things she never would have done had she been in her right mind. And with Brad of all guys.

But by God it was so good...

She gripped the hem of her nightshirt, which was still shoved up over her breasts, and pulled it down to her thighs to cover herself. Shocked by what had happened, she drew her knees to her chest, unable to stifle the low, tortured groan sounding in her throat as she buried her face in her hand. How would she ever face him? Then it occurred to her that he was going to be just as mortified as her when he woke up. As she mulled that over, there was another part of her, a small part that wondered—hoped—he'd crawled in here because he wanted her.

The feel of Brad's palms closing over hers—the same calloused palms that touched her body so eagerly last night—had her sucking in a sharp breath.

"Hey," he said, his voice soft, his eyes questioning as they pulled her hands from her face. "Are you okay?" he asked, looking sleepy, tousled and so damn sexy it took effort to keep her thoughts focused.

"Brad," she began, but had no idea what to say. "I...I..."

"Madison," he whispered, a frown knitting his brows together as his glance went from her to the mussed sheet. "Wait." He ran his hands through his hair and briefly pinched his eyes shut. "Did we...?"

She sat there, barely able to think let alone answer. She'd thought she was dreaming, thought she was simply having another one of her Brad fantasies, but from the wetness between her legs to the soreness of her muscles she knew it hadn't been a dream at all.

She'd had sex with Brad. Hard, hot, fast sex.

"Fuck," Brad groaned. "I'm sorry. Jesus Christ, I'm sorry, Madison. I thought..." he stopped talking while he pulled the sheet over his early morning erection, then started again with, "And I didn't even use a condom. Shit, I *always* use a condom."

Coming to his rescue she said, "It's okay, I'm on the pill and I'm clean."

"I'm clean too." He scrubbed his hand over his face, his brow knitted together in deep concern.

"And I get that you thought I was someone else."

His head jerked up, a confused look came over his face. "What? No. That's not what I meant."

She started to inch away, keeping the sheets tight against her. "I'd better go."

"Madison, wait. I didn't think you were someone else. Why would you say that?"

"Brad, this never should have happened."

"I know. It's my fault. I went to get a drink and forgot you were in here." Looking disgruntled and completely troubled he said, "I should have listened when you said those drugs knocked you out. I took two and chugged a beer." He shrugged and she could tell he was trying to lighten her mood when he said, "At least our colds seem to be better."

She picked at an invisible piece of lint, her hands shaking slightly, and when she went quiet, he scrubbed his chin, all humor gone from his face. "I'm sorry. It shouldn't have happened. It was a mistake."

"Yeah, it was a mistake," she whispered, her throat tightening as she mentally kicked herself. Brad didn't want her and in his drug-induced state probably thought he was crawling between the sheets with one of his perfectly-put-together brazen women.

But oh how I acted so brazen last night.

Her hair spilled forward and her stomach tightened with apprehension. She trembled despite the warmth of the body next to her.

"Are you okay?"

"No, I'm not okay."

Brad exhaled slowly, and raked his hands through his hair, mussing it even more. "Shit. We have to tell Jonah."

Madison's head came back with a start. "Tell Jonah? Why would we tell Jonah?"

His muscles flexed as he pinched the bridge of his nose. "Because he's my brother and I'm not going to keep something like this from him. I never thought you'd want to either."

"Brad?"

"Yeah."

"Pull the sheet up."

He dipped his head and she tried not to follow his gaze, tried not to stare at his growing erection, or the delicious way it was climbing out from beneath the sheet like it was ready for round two.

"Oh right." He pulled the sheet to his waist but she wished he'd cover himself to his neck. The sight of his naked chest, and hard abdominal muscles were making her mouth water.

"Okay, so what's the game plan then?" he asked when he had himself somewhat decent.

"Game plan?"

"How are we going to tell Jonah?"

Feeling antsy and frustrated she wrung the sheets between her hands. "I told you. Jonah never has to know what happened."

"Jesus, Madison. We owe it to him." His brow furrowed. "After all...you two are..."

"We're what?"

"Living together."

"So?"

"So...I think if you two are a couple then it's only right that you should tell him. If you don't want to do it I will. I'll just explain it was an accident, that I stumbled in here by mistake, and because I was so whacked out on cough medication, I thought I was dreaming when I...when we...you know... That way he'll be pissed at me and not you."

"Brad, you're not making any sense. Why would Jonah care what we did?"

He threw his hands up in the air like he was exasperated, and his sheet slipped a bit. "Because he's your boyfriend, that's why."

"What are you talking about?"

"Well, I assumed..."

She pulled the sheet to her neck. "Well, you assumed wrong. Jonah and I are friends. All we've ever been is friends."

Brad sat up next to her, the headboard creaking as he settled himself against it. He aimed those gorgeous blue eyes of his her way. "You've got to be fucking kidding me."

"Why would I kid about that?"

"So you and my brother." He paused and waved to the mussed sheets. "You're not...?"

She frowned and gave a quick shake of her head, her hair flying around her face. "No, we're not."

His mouth curved, a new gleam lighting his eyes. "You never have?"

"No."

He raked his hand through his hair. "Holy shit."

"What?"

"So then we have nothing to be sorry for."

"Well," she said, her rattled brain trying to keep up with his erratic train of thought.

Excitement moved over his face as he inched closer. "And there is no reason we can't do it again."

With her thoughts in turmoil, still trying to deal with what had happened between them, and why he thought she and Jonah were an item, she was having trouble following the conversation. "Do what again?"

"This."

"This?" she asked, realization dawning. "As in have sex again?" she squeaked out, her heart racing, confident that last night's cold and medication must have rattled her brain, because no way could Brad really be suggesting what she thought he was suggesting. When he nodded, rather enthusiastically, she gave a confused shake of her head. "You want to have sex again?"

"Hell yeah."

"With me?"

When he laughed she acknowledged the flare of desire between her legs then she acknowledged something else—the way he was inching closer, his eyes skirting over her covered body.

"Of course with you."

Her hand went to her hair to smooth it, and as she resisted reaching for her glasses, she was thankful that she'd forgotten her bite plate at home. "I just...I never thought you..."

"So what do you say, Madison?" He pushed his hands through her hair and cupped the back of her neck. "Do you want to sleep with me again?"

She swallowed, hardly able to believe what she was hearing. "I...I don't sleep with just anybody," she said for lack of anything else as she tried to wrap her brain around this unexpected turn of events.

He stroked the back of her neck with the soft pad of his finger and goose bumps broke out on her flesh. He inched closer until the scent of his skin overwhelmed her, and pitched his voice low, too low, and countered, "I'm hardly just anybody."

Every nerve in her body came alive and when she pushed her legs out straight, it pulled the sheet with her, exposing more of his rock-hard body. "We've never even been on a real date, never had dinner together," she blurted out. "Heck, we never even kissed." Although there was that kiss in the bathroom. But that was only because he had a concussion, right? When he gave her a grin, like he too was remembering the bathroom incident, she said, "I mean, not really."

Catching her off guard, he leaned in to her, and the second he closed his soft lips over hers, a whirlwind of sensations whipped through her. Her blood burned hotter, her nipples tightened and everything inside her urged her to go for it. Have wild, crazy sex with Brad. His tongue moved into her mouth, and she moaned, resisting the urge to pinch herself because how could this really be happening. A tremble moved through her as his mouth pressed hungrily, and deep between her legs, her pussy grew warm, slick, preparing for him again.

He inched back. "And you're wrong, when we've eaten together many times growing up. And just last night we shared a pizza."

Trying not to sound as breathless as she felt, she said, "It's not the same."

He pushed her hair back and his nostrils flared as he put his nose near her neck and breathed her in. "I like it when you smell like me."

"It's your deodorant," she explained. "I didn't have any yesterday so I used yours."

He angled his head, like he was processing that, then said, "It's more than that. I'm all over you."

Oh God, and how I want him all over her again!

Maybe she should go for it. Maybe she should have sex with him again. But then another thought hit. Last night was wild, crazy, and uninhibited because they'd both thought it was a dream. If she said yes to this, would Brad slow things down? She always took him for a guy who'd want to take his time to strip his woman bare and leave the lights on so he could look at inch of her body.

Before she could speak he said, "You're right, though."

"I'm right?"

"About the pizza and the meals we shared when we were young. Let me take you on a date tonight. A proper date at a nice restaurant, with a proper ending."

Oh God...

"A proper ending?"

He gave her a sheepish look as he placed his big hand over her stomach and splayed his fingers. "Yeah, you at least have to give me a chance to do this right."

Her pulse leapt thinking about the way he'd touched her, the way he'd buried his face in her pussy and licked her until she came. "You mean you did it wrong?"

He laughed. "Well sort of. I thought I was dreaming, so last night was kind of all about me. All about what I wanted." Intense blue eye full of heat and promise locked on hers. "I want to make sure you get what you want to."

"Oh, believe me, I did," she blurted out without thinking.

He grinned. "That's good to hear. But still, I want to take my time with you. I want to see every inch of you, kiss every inch of you."

As she thought about him taking his time with her, *seeing* and *kissing* every inch of her, her body tightened with unease. "Brad, I don't know—"

"I do." He grinned. "What's the harm in two friends having a little fun?"

Her mind raced. She knew Brad was a one-night kind of

guy and wasn't into relationships, not anymore, so what was he really asking of her. One more time. Two? Ten?

She wasn't sure, but it did beg the question, what did she want out of this? Well, she knew what she wanted but it wasn't like Brad wanted a long-term relationship with her. Honestly, he hadn't even noticed her before seeing her dressed in her tight work clothes that made her look sexy, confident...brazen. Like the kind of woman he gravitated toward. Clearly, that was the girl he wanted, considering he'd never shown interest before that. Despite the fact that she wanted long term, there was no way she could present Made-Up Madison forever. Eventually the real Madison would show through—the Madison who went without makeup and instead wore a bite plate, glasses and baggy, unflattering clothes—the Madison who would undoubtedly send Brad running for the hills because underneath the façade she was so not his type.

"What exactly are you asking me? To have sex with you again tonight?"

As if privy to her innermost thoughts, he said, "Yes, and every night for the rest of the month."

"One month?"

"I ship out in one month, so until then, why don't we just have some fun together?"

As she took a moment to chew on that, it occurred to her that she *could* do Made-Up Madison for thirty days. She could pretend to be something she wasn't for one month, and then when the fun ended and he shipped out, behind closed doors she could let her hair down and go back to being herself. After all, this was a once in a lifetime offer and she'd be a fool to turn it down, right?

"So what do you say, Madison. Do you want to spend the next thirty days having sex with me?"

5

"What the hell is going on between you and Brad?" Sophie asked in a hushed voice, her blonde brows furrowing as she hip-checked the cash register door to slam it shut.

After restocking the muffin tray, Madison quietly slid the glass panel closed, her stomach in turmoil as her best friend relentlessly grilled her. Buying herself a bit of time, Madison waited for the customer at the counter to step away and find a seat before she turned to her friend.

She ran her hands over her apron, lowered her voice and whispered, "I told you. He's going to stay in Jonah's room for the next month while Jonah is away. That way he can work on the repairs around here without having to travel back and forth so much." Rambling on, she waved her hands toward the ceiling, to where there were water stains. "There was a lot of damage done because of the flood. We're actually lucky to be open after yesterday's fiasco. If it wasn't for Brad getting the pipes and coil fixed, there is no way I could be up and running."

Brad...

God, just saying his name out loud, not to mention the fact that he'd be sleeping in the room next to hers for thirty glorious days, had heat moving through her body and her cheeks flushing from want.

Sophie hastily peeled off her latex gloves and set them next to the cash register. When she turned back to face Madison, she shot her a challenging look, the narrowing of her big brown eyes a clear indication that she knew Madison was hedging the truth and she wasn't one bit pleased about it.

"Yeah, I know what you told me, but did you forget how well I know you and how easy you are to read?" She crooked her index finger and held her ground. "So spill."

Madison glanced around, and from the curious looks on a few customers' faces, she had no doubt they overhead Sophie's comment. Working to keep the telltale grin from her face, and knowing this was neither the time nor place to be talking about her sex life she began, "Sophie—"

Sophie cut her off and widened her stance. "Go sell that crap to someone else. Jesus, Madison. Something is going on between you two. I can feel it." She waved her hand toward the patrons chatting quietly amongst themselves in the small bakery. "Hell, everyone in this place can feel it."

As Madison watched the lunch crowd drink coffee and eat pastries, she decided to keep Sophie dangling a little longer. She blinked innocently. "Feel what?"

Sophie waved her hand between Madison and the staircase that Brad had taken moments ago, a duffle bag and tool box in hand as he prepared to settle himself in for the next month. "The tension between you two."

Knowing she could never keep anything from her friend, especially one who was training to be a psychologist, Madison moved toward the kitchen area at the back of the bakery, out of sight of the patrons. She took the cakes out of the fridge and filled a decorating pen with icing as Sophie continued to glare at her.

"Look," Madison said, "I have no idea what you're talking about."

Sophie exhaled a frustrated breath. "Every time he walks by, your body sparks and you look like you're going to go off like one of the Fourth of July fireworks."

"Speaking of the Fourth, I really need to get working on those cupcakes for the band."

"Madison, tell me!"

"Okay, fine." Madison was ready to explode from the excitement bubbling up inside her. "If you really must know."

"Of course I must know," she blurted out.

Madison laughed and put her finger to her lips. "Shh." She glanced over Sophie's shoulder to make sure none of the customers were listening, then lowered her voice and said, "We had sex."

Sophie's eyes widened and her mouth fell open. She blinked twice then a third time. "Holy shit, Madison. I knew it. I knew something was going on. When...how?"

"As for when, it was last night. As for how, well, you should remember the how from Mr. Pincher's health class."

Sophie laughed. "Believe me I know *how*, but what I want to know is how it happened between you two. I'm mean, come on." She paused and shrugged her shoulders. "I knew you always liked him, but he always treated you like his kid brother's friend."

"Well, to be honest, it was kind of an accident."

"An accident?" Sophie scoffed. "What, did he fall on top of you and his penis accidently slid in or something?"

Madison grinned and then felt herself warm all over when she remembered their collision in the bathroom. Her mind momentarily drifted, reliving the feel of his strong, calloused hands on her back, holding her tight as she squirmed on top of him. She swallowed, her skin tightening all over, the hairs on her arms standing on end, charging with enough volatile electricity to run her bake ovens for days on end.

"There you go again," Sophie said. "You're giving off sparks. Keep it up and you're going to set this place on fire."

"I just... I can't..."

"What you can't do is stop grinning."

"I know I should, but I really can't make myself stop." She wrapped her arms around herself. "It was, oh God, it was amazing."

"Oh, believe me I can tell," Sophie said. "But what I want to know is how this accident happened?"

Madison quickly relayed the details, telling her friend about their sleeping arrangements, the cold medications, the beer Brad had chased the pills with, and how he'd become disoriented and accidently crawled into his bed.

Sophie threw her hands up in the air. "Now why can't I ever have an accident like that? Mine usually involve fiberglass casts and broken bones." Her eyes sparkled. "Speaking of bones..."

"Sophie," Madison admonished with a laugh, not about to give away too many details.

"Fine." She exhaled slowly and continued to probe. "At least tell me what happened after you both woke up and realized it wasn't a dream?"

"We were mortified at first, naturally, but after we talked about it, we decided that for the next month, we'd continue to have sex." Madison shrugged. "It's no big deal."

"From the color in your cheeks, I'm guessing it was a *big* deal."

Madison couldn't help but laugh, because Sophie was right, it was a *big* deal, in more ways than one.

Sophie curled up one lip and planted her hands on her

hips. "But why only one month? Why not until...whatever. Why the time limit? Does his dick turn into a pumpkin after thirty days or something? "

"Because," Madison began, "he's joining a convoy next month, and well..." She let her words fall off, not wanting to talk about the real reason she couldn't go past one month. But when Sophie frowned, Madison knew she could never keep anything from her friend, and it had nothing to do with the psychology degree Sophie was working on either. It was because back in the day, Sophie had always used a tender hand to dry the tears when the bullies struck. And Jonah, well, Jonah never used a gentle hand when he stood up for her.

"Madison, come on," Sophie said. "You're beautiful. Any guy would want you."

"Well, I don't know about that, but we're going on a date tonight," she said, hoping to change the subject.

"A date huh? Where is he taking you?"

"Beats me. It could be Chuck E. Cheese's for all I know."

"I somehow doubt it. He strikes me as a guy who knows how to take care of his woman."

Unable to wipe the silly grin off her face, Madison smiled, remembering all the delicious way he'd taken care of her last night.

Sophie pursed her lips and glanced at Madison's work clothes. "What are you going to wear?"

Madison quickly sobered and bit the inside of her cheek. When she wasn't in comfy clothes, she was in business suits, which hardly seemed suitable for a date with Brad, especially if they did end up at Chuck E. Cheese. "I was thinking maybe you'd help me with that. Brad dates certain types of women and for the next month I'll need..."

Sophie's eyes lit. "I know exactly what you need. There's a

nice boutique that opened just around the corner. Let's hit it after the lunch crowd dies down and find some clothes to showcase that gorgeous body of yours."

A wave of unease moved through her, Brad's words coming back to haunt her.

I want to take my time with you. I want to see you.

As if sensing her sudden distress, Sophie said. "He wouldn't have slept with you if he didn't like you, Madison."

"I told you it was an accident."

"Maybe so, but why do you think he wants to do it again...and again?"

Because she was wild, wanton, uninhibited in bed...like the women he was used to. And sure to God, for one month, she could continue to be that woman. As long as she managed to keep him from turning on the lights when they were between the sheets. Otherwise he might just see the real Madison.

The bell over the door jangled, and Madison was thankful for the distraction. She didn't need another lecture on self-confidence from her friend. Lord knows she'd had enough of them over the years, and they did little to help her with her body image issues.

Madison gestured toward the front of the bakery. "You better get out there; you have a customer."

"Fine, I'm going, but let me ask. Why do you think he's sleeping with you?"

"I don't know. Because he likes sex?"

Sophie pointed a finger at her. "Well, of course he likes sex, he's a man. But he wants it with you, and you know why? It's because he likes you."

What he liked was the carefree woman she was in her sleep, one without issues or hang-ups, but she didn't want to get into that with Sophie.

"And you never know, maybe sleeping together could lead to something more."

"This is just sex, Sophie. Just for one month." Madison knew better than to hope for more. Brad had never gotten over his ex's betrayal. It had left him bitter and resentful, unwilling to put himself out there again. Since the breakup, he went from woman to woman, bed to bed, and Madison, well, she could never be the kind of girl he was really attracted to and gravitated toward, at least not for more than thirty days.

Sophie shrugged. "I know this couple who started sleeping…"

Sophie's voice fell off at the sound of Brad's heavy boots hitting the bottom step. Their conversation died an abrupt death when they both turned to see him coming their way. As if sensing he was interrupting them, his glance tennis balled between the two of them.

"Everything okay?" he asked.

"Yeah, Sophie was just about to head back to the counter and I'm getting ready to decorate these cakes."

Brad nodded, then focused on Madison, his eyes serious. "Do you have a second?"

"Yeah, why, what's up?"

As soon as the question left her mouth, Sophie snickered, and asked, "Yeah, what's up, Brad?" Jesus, Madison was going to kill her friend when she got her alone.

He gestured overhead. "There's something I want to show you."

"I just bet there is," Sophie whispered before disappearing down the hall.

———

Holy Christ!

Brad took one look at Madison and damn near swallowed his tongue. He hadn't seen her since earlier that afternoon, when he'd taken her upstairs to point out all the pipes in need of repair, and what he was seeing now rocked his world and completely threw him off kilter.

Standing outside Jonah's room, Brad leaned against the doorjamb and drove his hands into his pockets as she exited her bedroom. With a strange, almost apprehensive look on her face, she took a tentative step toward him, her palms flitting nervously over the black dress that accentuated her curves and had his cock rising to the occasion. Since she usually walked around in baggy clothes that hid her beautiful body, yet still inspired his imagination, it surprised him to see her in something so sexy, so revealing. Something that aroused his hunger and brought out another emotion in him, one he never wanted to feel again.

Jealousy.

He drove his hands deeper into his pockets in an attempt to shift his cock and wrestle it into submission, but when he caught her sweet cherry scent his efforts proved futile. What the hell was it about her in that dress that had him wanting to keep her here in the apartment, in his bed, so no other man could look at her? Early that morning, while lying in bed, they'd set the ground rules for this fling. Thirty days of sex, and nothing else. He'd be wise to remember that and keep all his other emotions in check because he wasn't looking for anything more. With the way Madison had readily agreed to the terms, it was clear that she wasn't either.

But goddammit, she was smoking hot.

Brad swallowed the saliva pooling on his tongue as he stared at her, but there was nothing he could do to stifle the moan crawling out of his throat or keep himself from murmuring, "Jesus..."

"What?" she asked, inching backward, obviously

mistaking his shock for something else. "Am I overdressed? Should I get changed?" She made a move to turn, mumbling something about Chuck E. Cheese and the dress being Sophie's idea.

"No, wait." He hurried out when he caught the distress in her voice. He took two measured steps toward her and grabbed her wrist to prevent her from fleeing. "It's just...I'm not used to seeing..." He let his words drift away and exhaled slowly before saying, "You look beautiful."

She gave him an odd look, dark lashes blinking quickly over big brown eyes, then she relaxed a bit and nodded. "So do you."

"Oh yeah?" he asked, looking at his shirt, tie and black dress pants. "No one has ever called me beautiful before." Still holding her hand, he rubbed his thumb over the inside of her wrist, gave her a wink and added, "Rugged, handsome and adorable for sure, and I've even heard sex god tossed around a time or two, but never beautiful."

Her grin reached her eyes and lit up her pretty face. Jesus, she was gorgeous, which made him wonder why she didn't have a horde of men pounding down her door, or why she'd agree to one month of sex with a train wreck like him when she could have her pick of guys.

"Adorable? I think you might have made that one up," she teased. "You're hardly adorable."

He stepped closer, crowding her. When she wet her lips, he noticed the rapid-fire pulse in her neck. He dipped his head and asked, "So you're saying you agree that I'm sex god?"

She crinkled her nose. "I never said that."

He laughed and wrapped a long strand of her dark hair around his finger. He gave a little tug, and teased, "You mean...yet."

"Well, I suppose you do have thirty days to convince me,"

she ribbed in return, her words reminding him of the parameters they set in place.

He felt a shiver move through her, and while he wanted to scoop her into his arms and carry her right back into her bedroom where he could make up for last night and do right by her for the next month, he knew they had a reservation waiting. Besides, he wanted to take her on a real date. After fucking her like a goddamn rutting animal, she deserved at least that much from him. "Now, come on. We don't want to be late."

Thirty minutes later, they stood inside the doors of one of the fanciest restaurants in town. Since he was a fast-food kind of guy, he'd only been to the restaurant once, just last year when his buddy Cole Sullivan and his new wife, Gemma, had invited all their friends to celebrate their engagement party. He shook his head, hardly able to believe how many of his comrades were either married, getting married, and had kids on the way. Honestly, though, there was a side of him that kind of resented what the others had. But he'd long ago resigned himself to the fact that love, commitment and monogamy weren't in the cards for him.

"This place is gorgeous." Madison smoothed her hands over her stomach and took it all in.

Brad spoke to the maître d and then slipped his arm around Madison's back to guide her to their table, a nice cozy spot in the corner. After they placed their drink order, he turned his full attention to his date. When he found her staring at him, a small smile on her face, he angled his head and asked, "What?"

She toyed with the stem of her wine glass, then glanced around the dimly lit restaurant. "I'm impressed."

"Of course, it's no Chuck E. Cheese's," he teased lightly. "And every now and then a guy's gotta get out of his fatigues and get cleaned up."

"I like you in your work wear, but you do clean up nicely."

He was about to tell her he liked her in her comfy work wear too, and how he'd like to peel that apron off her hips and tie her up with the long strings, but stopped when a contemplative look passed over her face. Her eyes left his to travel to his shoulder, then lower. Without her gaze every leaving his body, she reached into her purse and pulled out her lip balm. As she applied it, he inhaled sharply, her scent hardening his dick and burning his blood.

As sexual energy sparked between them, he croaked out, "You shouldn't do that."

"Do what?" She recapped her balm and tossed it back into her purse.

"Look at me like that when you're putting that stuff on your lips."

"Why?"

He clenched his jaw, his nostrils flaring. "Because it makes me want to bend you over this table and taste you."

"Oh," she said, a mixture of surprise and delight back-lighting her dark eyes. "I didn't realize how much you like cherry."

"I love cherry."

Her eyes widened when she got the gist of what he was saying. "Oh," she said again.

The server came with their drinks, and Brad shifted in his seat, his knees bumping hers under the table. Once they were alone again, they sipped wine and looked over the menu, but his appetite for food was long gone. There was only one thing he was interested in putting in his mouth tonight.

"Hey, Brad," someone said from behind. "I thought that was you." He turned and climbed to his feet when he found Cole and Gemma coming his way. Brad gave Gemma a kiss on the cheek and exchanged a handshake with his buddy, Cole.

"I'm surprised to see you here." Cole's glance left his and moved to Madison. "Oh...I didn't realize..."

"You remember Madison, don't you?" Brad asked.

"Yeah, I, ah, of course. Don't she and Jonah...?" He paused and turned to Brad, the expression on his face letting his comrade know he needed help before he put his damn military issue boot in his mouth.

"Yeah, she and Jonah go way back."

"Friends since childhood," Madison piped in. "And current roommates."

"Well, it's nice to meet you, Madison," Gemma said, coming around from behind her husband and holding her hand out for a shake.

Madison's eyes lit when she saw Gemma's belly. "How are you feeling?"

"Like a damn beached whale."

After they laughed, Gemma turned to Brad and poked him in the chest. "You are still coming, right?"

Brad groaned. "Come on, Gemma. Don't make me."

"Forget it, pal." Cole drove his thumb into his chest. "If I have to be there, you have to be there."

"What happened to traditions?" Brad asked. "The girls go to the baby shower, and the guys get shit-faced drunk at the bachelor party."

"It's not the way it's done anymore," Gemma said, rubbing her belly with one hand while she wagged a warning finger at him with another. "I expect you there three weeks from this Saturday. I expect all her uncles to be there." Even though they weren't really related, the guys were all a brotherhood, treating one another's families like they were their own, which meant in some twisted way he was the baby's uncle and therefore had to go to the damn baby shower.

Gemma turned to Madison and gave her a big smile. "And

bring your friend. It will give me and the girls a chance to get to know her better."

As he groaned, Jack Myers came up behind Cole. "Come on. Our table is ready," he said, but when he noticed Brad standing there and Madison seated in the chair across from his, Jack shot him a warning look.

Clearly they all assumed his kid brother and Madison were a couple. Hell, how could he blame them. Up until this morning he'd thought so too. He wanted to clarify things, but what was he supposed to say... "Oh, we're just friends but decided it would be fun to fuck for the next month." As he stood there with his mouth open, thinking it best to keep their relationship a secret, Jack's date slid in beside him.

She gave Brad a dazzling smile and smoothed her long hair from her face. Big diamond earrings glistened as she turned her gaze turned to Madison.

"Hello...*Maddy*," she said, shortening and dragging out her name as a small grin tugged at her painted lips.

Brad's glance went from Jack's date to Madison. "You two know." He stopped speaking when he saw the pained look on Madison's face.

"Sarah," Madison responded quietly as she sank a little farther down in her seat, conveying without words how uncomfortable she was.

What the hell?

Brad quickly exchanged a look with his comrades, who seemed to taste Madison's tension every bit as much as he did, so when Jack wrapped his arm around Sarah's waist and said, "We should get moving before they give our table away," Brad was grateful for the interference.

Once the crew disappeared, he dropped back into his chair, noting the distance look in Madison's eyes.

"So how do you know Sarah?"

Madison dug into the bread the waiter had delivered and said, "High school."

As he considered the venomous look Sarah shot Madison, the wheels began turning. "Let me guess, ex-girlfriend of Jonah's? Hates you because you two were, and still are, tight?"

"No, her hate goes deeper than that."

When she reached for another piece of bread, he closed his hands over hers. "What's going on?"

She went quiet for a moment, like she was remembering something from the past, then she said quietly, "She was one of the mean girls."

"You mean—"

"I mean she picked on me."

"Picked on you? Why would anyone pick on you?"

Madison put her elbows on the table, and folded her hands in front of her face, making it hard for him to see her. With her expression veiled, she said, "Because I was fat, which makes me an easy target for girls like her."

"Fat?" He removed her hands from her face. "What are you talking about?"

"She and her friends called me Fatty Maddy. She just left the fatty off this time, but the meaning was still there."

"Jesus, Madison, I had no idea."

"How could you? You were older and hung out in a different crowd."

Anger boiled his blood. "Yeah, but Jonah didn't."

"Don't worry. He always stood up for me."

"Good." He relaxed slightly. "Otherwise I was going to have to beat the crap out of him when he returned."

That pulled a small smile from her. "You were a good big brother, Brad. You still are. You taught him to fight for what was right and for what was worth fighting for."

Just then the server came with their food. As he watched Madison adjust her napkin over her lap and pick up her fork, he felt a wave of protectiveness move through him. He didn't like the idea of anyone hurting her, and in that instance, as she looked up at him with vulnerability on her face, he made a vow to himself. Not only was he taking over his brother's room, he was also going to take over a few more of Jonah's *best friend* duties. Which meant while Madison was on his clock, no one was ever going to hurt her again.

6

Madison shifted restlessly in the seat beside Brad as they drove home from the restaurant. She had no idea why she'd revealed something so personal to him at dinner. She never talked about her high school days with anyone, least of all a date. Then again, Brad wasn't just anyone. It was odd though, after she'd opened up to him, something inside him seemed to shift. He'd always had a protective side, and had always taken care of his brother, but now seemed a little more protective of her.

Maybe she was just imagining it. Maybe he'd dragged his seat closer to hers in the restaurant, and pulled her against him and out of Sarah's line of sight as he led her from the establishment for other reasons, reasons that had nothing to do with being protective, and more to do with his plans for later that night.

Proper ending...

She gulped and shot a glance his way. He turned to look at her, and his smile was so boyish, so adorable, that her heart missed a beat.

Cupping her hands, she quickly tore her gaze away, hardly

able to believe what they were going to do next. Sure they had sex last night, but this was different because this time they'd both be fully conscious, which made it feel like the first time for her.

He pulled into her driveway and killed the ignition. Madison gripped the door handle and tried not to appear nervous or apprehensive as she climbed from the cab. Brad met her at the front of the truck and slipped his arm around her back.

Her entire body came alive as they walked toward her bakery door. She slipped in her key and Brad pushed open the door. After she stepped inside, she listened to the bolt slide home, and a quiver raced down her spine.

He gripped her hand, but she stilled, and gestured with a nod toward the kitchen area in the back. "I...uh...there are a few things I need to check on."

He dipped his head, his gaze moving over her face. His voice came out a little deeper, a little sexier when he asked, "Do you need help?"

"No, it's okay. You go on up. I'll be there shortly."

"Okay. I need to check on the pipes anyway."

After he disappeared up the stairs, Madison darted into the back room, to where she left her makeup kit earlier that evening. Even though she wanted to take out her contacts, put her hair into a ponytail and slip into something comfortable, she fixed her curls, reapplied her mascara and touched up her lipstick. Then she stood back to give herself a once over in the mirror. Not quite comfortable with the way her clothes showcased her body, she spun around and exited the bathroom. As she walked by the counter, she checked on the cakes she'd made that day, hoping they were cool enough to be put away. She grabbed an apron, not wanting to dirty her new dress, and slid the trays into the fridge.

When she turned back around, she found Brad standing

at the foot of the stairs, a grin on his face as he watched her. Dressed in nothing but his jeans, his hard, naked torso pulling all her focus, he braced his hands on the paint-chipped doorframe over his head.

"Hey," he murmured, his glance dropping to her apron. "Are you coming up?"

Forcing her wobbly knees to work, she walked toward him, and tried to sound casual. "Just finished."

"Oh no, Madison," he murmured, his eyes darkening as he pulled her against him, the feel of his hard cock pressing into her stomach sucking the oxygen from her lungs. He put one finger under her chin and lifted it until he brought them face-to-face. "We're just getting started."

His lips came down on hers, and she sank into him, enjoying the flavor of his mouth as his tongue slipped inside to tangle with hers. He kissed her long and hard, and when he increased the pressure, she could feel the tension rising in him.

The pounding of his heart matched hers, and with his lips still moving, ravaging her mouth, he mumbled, "I need you naked, sweetheart. There are so many things I need to do to you."

She moaned, and it seemed to do something to him. His breathing changed, came faster, heavier, and before she knew what was happening, he scooped her up in his arms, taking full control of her and the situation.

She felt a quick flash of panic, and gave a little squeal, but she had to admit, she loved this take-charge side of the sexy soldier.

A shiver of anticipation moved through her as he carried her to her room. He lowered her to her feet just inside her bedroom door, then kicked it shut, drowning them both in darkness. Light from the streetlamps outside her window slanted against the wall through the crack in her drapes. It gave sufficient illumination to see his features as he moved closer.

Equal amounts of pleasure and unease skittered along her spine as he pushed against her and backed her up against the door. Taking both her hands in his, he pinned them above her head, and pushed a knee between her legs to widen them.

She bit back a breathy moan when she caught the intent look in his eyes as they moved over her face. His gaze visually caressed her, a fire brewing in their stormy depths. "Baby, I need you naked. I need to see you."

Her pulse raced and her nerves flared hot. While she liked the idea of getting naked with him, she wasn't keen on him gazing at her bare body. "Brad," she started, but his mouth closed over hers, swallowing her protests. As his tongue thrashed against hers, he let go of her hands and ran his palm down her sides, stroking the outer edges of her breasts. He pulled her away from the door and slipped a hand around her back. He untied her apron and tossed it onto the bed, then his hands went to her zipper. The hiss from him sliding it down her back cut through the quiet, and after he released it, the slip of material fell to her ankles. Even though she was under the cover of darkness, she felt a little exposed, and a little uneasy as she stood before him in nothing but her lacy bra and panties.

A groan crawled out of his throat as he shaped her curves in the dark, and without giving him a chance to go for the light, she slipped past him, and grabbed his hand, drawing him to her bed. She put shaky hands on his chest, enjoying the feel of his muscles beneath her palms.

"But, baby, I need to see you," he murmured into her ear as he dragged her closer. His arms circled her back to release the hook on her bra, freeing her breasts.

She went up on her toes and pressed her mouth to his, her

fingers sliding around his neck to hold him close, overwhelmed by the heat in his body, the raw hunger inside her.

Her bare breasts pushed against his hard chest, and he slid his hands down her back until he reached the crest of her buttocks. "Jesus, your skin is soft," he murmured into her mouth. Then he inched back and inhaled. "And you smell so fucking good."

She ran her nails over his shoulders and his breath came ragged as his body trembled. His mouth found hers again as his fingers curled around the band of her panties. Her skin moistened while some small working part of her brain reminded her that this was Brad. Brad! She was about to have sex with the guy she'd been crazy about for years—again.

But all coherent thought fled when his mouth left her. He buried his face in the curve of her neck, his tongue burning her flesh as he trailed a lazy path downward. Blood pounded through her as his breath tickled her skin. His mouth found her nipple and she gave a broken gasp, her hands going to his head to hold him to her. As he paid homage to her breasts, her thoughts scattered, her brain concentrating only on the delicious points of pleasure and nothing else.

"So good," she murmured in an unsteady voice.

He swirled his hot, skilled tongue around her hard bud, his knuckles brushing over her pelvis as he continued to toy with the lace on her panties. He body stirred, no... *trembled*...almost violently, and she rocked her hips, need urging her on. She arched her back and moved against him, and when a growl ripped from his throat, she crushed her hands in his hair, her cries of pleasure matching his.

His inched back and looked at her in the dark as his hand slipped inside her panties. He ran his finger along her slit, and her clit quivered. Feeling a little out of control, her breath came fast and her knees weakened.

"Please, Brad...I need you inside me," she begged, her

hands moving urgently over his body as she ached for him to take her hard and fast, a repeat performance of last night.

"Oh, I don't think so," he murmured, his hot breath spilling over her naked flesh.

Her body tensed when he backed away, sexual tension hanging heavy between them. Wondering if he was suddenly having second thoughts, she swallowed hard, her mind racing. But before she could ask what was going on, he said, "Tonight I'm wide awake, and we're going to take it nice and slow."

Even though she could hear the urgency in his words, feel the tension in his body when he dropped to his knees to press his mouth into her stomach, he continued with his slow seduction. When she gripped his head, he nudged her backward until her knees hit the bed, then he did something that completely surprised her. Alarmed her.

Aroused her.

"Oh, God," she cried out when he shackled her hands behind her back in one of his and reached for the apron he'd tossed away earlier.

He quickly tied her hands, pulling her shoulders back and forcing her breasts to jut out even more in the dim light. But she couldn't think about how exposed she felt, not when it felt so deliciously naughty to be tied up by him, his to do with as he pleased.

"What are you...?" she asked breathlessly.

"Anything I want." He slid his fingers between the knot in the apron strings and her wrist. "Move your hands."

Madison wiggled her hands, obeying the deep command on instinct. Her body responded with a shudder as Brad showed her a side of himself that she'd never seen before, a side that excited her beyond anything she'd ever known.

With a grunt of satisfaction, he stood up, and gave her a little nudge until she was sitting on the bed. As lamplight splashed across her mattress, he looked down at her silhouette for a long time, longer than was comfortable.

"You are so beautiful," he murmured.

She shifted, hardly able to believe the way he was looking at the outline of her curves. God, no man had ever looked at her like that before. It made her feel wanted, desired, and maybe even a little sexy. As her caught her lip between her teeth, his nostrils flared and in a tone that was both soft and commanding, he ordered, "Widen your legs for me."

Oh God.

Her heart beat madly, everything in his controlling voice thrilling her beyond belief. Her pussy moistened, damping her panties as she inched her legs open.

"More," he demanded.

She wiggled her hands in the bindings again, and that's when she realized the knot was loose enough for her to free her bound hands...*if she wanted to*.

As Brad stared at her, waiting for her compliance, she opened her legs even more. The warm scent of her arousal reached her nostrils as it saturated her small bedroom.

"That's a girl," Brad said, his voice unsteady.

Her chest heaved with a new kind of excitement when he sank to the floor and gripped her knees. His smile stretched wickedly when he shifted closer, positioning himself between her legs. She strained against the restraints. God, she wanted to touch him, to feel his corded muscles beneath her palms, but kept her hands behind her back, where he wanted them. Where *she* wanted them.

Her nerve endings came alive as he slid his hands up her thighs, coming perilously close to the spot that needed his touch. She made a sexy noise and squirmed.

He lifted his head, a gleam in his eyes when they met hers. "What is it, baby?" he asked, and her body flushed at the intimacy in his tone.

She licked her dry lips, and oddly enough could feel her inhibitions ebbing under his artful touch and ravenous gaze. She gave an impatient sigh and whispered, "I want...too slow...I need..."

A low chuckle rumbled in his throat and he dipped his head, and tugged her panties to the side. "Don't worry. I know what you need, and I plan to spend all night giving it to you."

His words alone nearly took her over the edge. She thrust her pelvis forward, a bold, daring move that surprised even her.

He lowered his head and breathed a kiss over her inner thigh. She gave a throaty purr and tried to jut her hips forward, to force his mouth to her pussy, but he gripped her waist to still her. Damn him!

"Brad. Please." she cried.

His tongue trailed higher, teasing the other edges of her nether lips, playing with her in ways that left her panting, crazed. He dragged the soft blade toward her core, then finally, *finally*, licked her hot spot.

That first sweet swipe of his tongue over her pussy damn near had her unraveling like a frayed pair of shorts. Heat spread over her skin, a tremor ripping through her as her clit filled with heated blood. Lost in the sensations, the amazing things this man could do with the wet tip of his tongue, she whimpered and moved against him. He stroked her gently, and small quakes began deep in her womb. As her skin grew tight, he pushed a thick finger inside, a deliciously snug fit that built the tension inside her.

Her walls gripped him hard, and she heard Brad draw in a shaky breath. He pushed his finger in and out of her, slow at first but then he picked up the pace as she grew slicker. As she moistened and his fingers easily slipped in and out of her, she heard heated curses coming from deep between her legs.

Female prowess welled up inside her. It was insane how much it thrilled her to see Brad coming unglued, because of her.

"You taste so fucking good," he murmured, then ran his tongue along the length of her crevice.

The pleasure was unreal, so damn exquisite, air rushed from her lungs and took every sane though with it.

"Don't stop," she cried out as he slowly coaxed an orgasm from her.

"Baby, I'm not going to stop," he assured her in a rough whisper, driving his fingers in a little deeper as his mouth devoured her pussy, running his teeth over her clit. A shiver racked her body, and a fever rose in her as he continued to take her higher and higher. As she hovered on the precipice, she took deep gulping breaths, and fell back on the bed, her hands tucked under her ass as he feasted on her.

Everything in the way he touched her was deeply intimate, highly erotic, and before she knew it pleasure raced through her veins as her muscles clenched tightly around him.

"Oh...Brad...so...good," she cried out.

"Jesus," he murmured, arousal edging his voice as she arched her back, raising her wet pussy to his mouth. He lapped at her as she rode out the waves of pleasure, her body tingling all over. When her spasms stopped, she exhaled slowly, and glanced at the man crawling out from between her legs.

With his mouth damp from her cream, and his eyes dark and intense, his hands went to the button on his dress pants. She watched, transfixed as he grabbed something from his pocket before he pushed his pants down his legs and kicked them away. Her glance went to his cock, and even though he'd been deep inside her last night, and she knew he was impressive, until this moment she had no idea just how impressive.

A growl sounded in his throat then he asked, "Are you ready for me?"

"Yes," she whispered. The streetlight splashed across his naked body, and she warmed all over at the gorgeous sight of his hard muscles. A shudder caught her off guard as he climbed over her, gripped her shoulders and moved her to the middle of the bed, her hands still tied behind her back. This time she squirmed out of the binding, needing in the most inexplicable ways to touch him in return

His mouth found hers as she wrapped her hands around his neck. "Baby, I want to make you come for me again, but this time I want to be inside you."

"Yes," she purred into his mouth, liking that idea very much.

He went back on his knees and gripped the band on her panties. His breath came a little harder as he slowly dragged them down her legs. He brought them to his nose and inhaled. "Mmmm, cherry," he murmured, then dropped them onto the floor. He shifted, and it gave her a moment of pause when he sheathed himself, considering they'd had unpro-tected sex already and he knew she was on the pill. But she lost all train of thought when he turned his attention back to her. He climbed up her body and positioned his cock at her opening.

"Tell me you want this."

"I want this," she managed to get out, and then feeling a little naughty and a whole lot brazen, lifted her hips upward in a futile attempt to force him inside.

"Jesus, don't do that."

"Don't do what?" she asked, feigning innocence.

"You know what you're doing and if you don't stop, I won't be able to go slow."

"Who says I want it slow?"

He shook his head, and pitched his voice low. "You really are a bad girl, aren't you?"

She lifted her hips again, his words encouraging her wicked behavior.

"Fuck, Madison."

"Exactly," she said, and as she reveled in the light-hearted, sexy banter between them, it occurred to her how fun he was to be with, how much she enjoyed this new, easy intimacy.

He angled his head and gave her a bad boy grin. "Okay. Let's fuck, then." He put all his body weight on top of her, gripped her legs to wrap them around his waist, and in one hard thrust, pushed all the way inside her.

She ran her nails along his back and gasped as he completely filled her. "Oh, my God," she cried out as she bit into his shoulder.

He drove into her, one hand going to her breast to knead it while he buried his mouth in the hollow of her neck.

He slammed hard, his muscles clenching and flexing as he took deep ragged breaths. She met each thrust, raising her hips to his. As their bodies came together she held him tight, reveling in the sensation. With his breath hot on her neck, she could feel him thicken inside her, knew he was so close to the edge.

The nerve endings in her clit screamed for attention and, as if knowing exactly what she needed, he slipped a hand between their bodies. Her breath caught, and her body trembled, a powerful orgasm taking her by surprise.

With her cream making her slicker and her muscles spasming around him, he pulled all the way out, took a sharp intake of breath, then drove back inside. His body stilled and he gripped her shoulders.

"I'm going to come, baby," he murmured, his voice husky with need. His eyes moved over her face and they exchanged a long, lingering look that nearly robbed her of her next breath. There was something so intimate, so profound in his expression, it seeped under her skin and touched her on a deeper level.

As he gave himself over to his climax, he dipped his head, his mouth settling possessively over hers. His palm went to her face, and his kiss was so tender, so steeped in desire, it did the weirdest things to her insides. Her lids fluttered right along with her heart and, working to ignore the emotions sweeping through her, she concentrated on the ripples moving onward and upward through her body.

His weight settled on top of her, and after a long moment he rolled to the side and discarded his condom. He dropped back down on the bed and put his arm around her to pull her close.

She took a fortifying breath and snuggled against his chest, a quiet, comfortable silence falling over them.

Once his breathing regulated and she was able to think with clarity again, she whispered, "Wow."

"Wow?" he asked, his tone playful as he looked at her. "That's it? Wow?"

"Okay, how about wow, that was amazing."

His expression was tender, hot and so damn adorable when he grinned at her, her heart tightened in her chest. "Aren't you leaving something off the end of that sentence?"

She shrugged even though she knew exactly what he was getting at. "Like what?"

"Like, 'Wow, that was amazing, Brad. You really are a sex god.'"

Unable to help herself she chuckled. "Well, I'm not so sure I'd go so far—"

"Oh no?" he said, cutting her off as he climbed over her and grabbed her legs to flip her onto her stomach. "Then you leave me no choice but to fuck you again, until you say it."

He grabbed a pillow and placed it under her hips, then ran

his hands over the swell of her backside before giving it a slap. A quiver moved through her as his fingers burned her skin in the most erotic ways.

"And if I don't say it?" she asked.

He put his mouth close to her ear and his playful words were full of promise when he whispered, "Oh, you will, baby, you will."

———

"Madison," Brad whispered, his heart tightening uneasily in his chest as he took in the gorgeous woman sleeping beside him.

Madison blinked her sleepy eyes open, confusion moving over her face when her glance met his. "Brad?" she asked. "What is it?"

"I have to go," he said quietly.

Her palm closed over his cheek, and the feel of her warm hand, not to mention the deep concern in her eyes, felt like an emotional sucker punch. Jesus, what was it about her that suddenly had him wanting more, had him thinking about long term? Even though everything in her touch, everything in the way she'd given herself over to him last night had him forgetting past hurts, and that commitment and monogamy weren't in the cards for him, they'd both agreed that this was a fling. And what if he did give himself over to the things he was feeling, and after thirty days she was ready to end this game they were playing? The last thing he wanted was another kick to the gut.

"What's wrong?" she asked.

He held up his cell phone. "It's Granddad. They called from the nursing home. He's not doing well. I have to go."

Leaping into action, she sat up, but kept a sheet wrapped around her body, hiding her nakedness from him. "Wait. I'm coming with you."

His heart squeezed as he gave her a nudge, forcing her to lie down again. "No, you don't have to do that. That's not why I woke you." He looked at her nightstand. "I wanted to leave a note but couldn't find a pen. I just didn't want you to wake up and wonder where I was." He tightened the bed sheet around her body, tucking her back in. "It's still early. You should try to get a few more hours sleep."

She smiled at him, a smile so full of emotion and warmth it messed with his head...and his heart. Ignoring his suggestion, she sat back up, and threw her legs over the side of the bed. "We'll take my car. I'll drive."

He opened his mouth, but understanding he really needed to get moving, he gave a resigned sigh, stood, and said, "I'm okay to drive."

With the sheet still wrapped tightly around her, she shooed him away. "It's okay, I'll drive, now go get dressed." She opened her dresser and pulled out a pair of panties and a bra, then she hurried to her closet. As she grabbed a pair of pants and a T-shirt, Brad went to his own room. He climbed into a clean pair of jeans and T-shirt and shoved his wallet into his pocket. When he came back and found Madison standing there, one hip to the side as she bent forward to run a brush through her long hair, his breath caught in his throat.

Her body stiffened when she heard him, then she pulled on a sweater and said, "Let's go."

As she breezed past him he wondered how she could pull off both sweet and sexy at the same time. He forced himself to clear his lusty thoughts; otherwise he might be tempted to take her again. And right now he had other more pressing matters at hand.

They hurried to her car and less than half an hour later, they stepped up to the counter at the nursing home. "I'm

Brad Crosby. I got a call about my grandfather, Chester Crosby."

The nurse nodded, then turned her focus to Madison. "Family only," she said.

Without even pausing, Brad slipped his arm around Madison's waist. "She is family."

She nodded. "Okay, follow me."

She led them down the hall toward his granddad's room and told them to have a seat outside assuring them both the doctors would be out to talk to them shortly. They both took a seat and as he worried for his grandfather, Madison took his hand.

"I'm sure he's going to be okay," she said.

Brad nodded and squeezed her hand. He'd sat outside his grandfather's room a time or two over the past year, but this time it felt oddly comforting to have Madison there with him.

"I know, but I like to be here anyway."

"Do they always call you?"

He nodded. "Yeah, I had the nurses put a note on his file to call if anything changes."

Emotions moved over her eyes. "Not only are you a good big brother, you're a good grandson too."

"Granddad was always there for me after Mom and Dad died. We sort of count on each other."

"You two have a special bond." The softness in her voice, and the way she nestled against him, felt like a healing balm to the soul. "That's nice, Brad."

"He'll be happy to see you," Brad said, attempting to change the subject before his emotions got the better of him. "He always liked you."

"I always liked him too."

"Just remember," he said cautiously. "He doesn't have the same filters as he used to." When she crinkled her brow he went on to explain, "He says things without thinking. It's the dementia."

Just then the doctor came out, and Brad stood. "How is he?"

"He's going to be fine. His heart began racing through the night, but we were able to stabilize it." He flipped through the pages on his clipboard. "I've given him something to help him sleep, so you won't have much time. Just be sure not to say anything to excite or upset him."

Brad nodded, captured Madison's hand and quietly moved into the room. He stepped up to the bed, his heart tightening as he took in the machines and oxygen tubes.

"Hey, Granddad," Brad said quietly.

"That you, Brad?" Chester asked, his eyes lighting as they turned Brad's way.

"Yeah, it's me," Brad said a bit louder, knowing his granddad was hard of hearing. "Doctor said you had a bit of trouble. Are you feeling better now?"

"I'm feeling fine. Dang nurses, I told them there was no need to call you. Hate to bother you."

"You're not bothering me," he assured him, even though he knew how happy the old man was to see him.

"Who's that with you?" He sat up a little in his bed, a smile on his face when he peered at Madison. "Why, is that little Madison Graham?"

Madison moved closer to Brad. "It's me," she said.

He gave a low whistle. "'Bout time you figured it out, girlie."

Brad stiffened then shot her a look to suggest she humor him.

"Figured what out, Granddad?"

"Jonah's a nice kid," he said, tsking. Then he wagged a finger toward Brad. "But I knew this boy was the one you always wanted. Couldn't hide that from me. No siree." He shook his head, a gleam in his eyes as he jerked his thumb toward Brad. "Took this fool long enough to figure it out, though. He can be dense sometimes, you know. He get's that from his grandmother's side. She had an uncle that wasn't all there either."

Brad laughed. "Did you just call me dense?"

"Brad?" he said, his voice suddenly turning serious as his mind shifted directions, as it quite often did.

"Yeah, Granddad? What is it?"

"Have you moved into the house yet, son?"

"Not yet," Brad hedged. "I'm still working on repairs."

That seemed to satisfy his granddad. He nodded. "Okay, but don't take too long. Before I go, I like to see it full of grandkids."

When his eyes slipped shut, Brad stood there for a moment longer, emotions choking him as he remembered his younger days at the old Victorian house Granddad had built by hand. He and Jonah and his mom and dad had spent a lot of time visiting, and both Brad and Jonah loved their overnight trips, especially when they were allowed to stay up late and watch trash television. The place held many happy memories for the entire Crosby family.

Brad had hedged the truth with his granddad. Even though he was fixing the place up, he had no intention of moving into it or filling it with kids. He actually planned to put it up for sale, but such news would only upset Chester, and that was the last thing Brad wanted to do. Where was the harm in letting him believe Brad was going to take up residency and fill the rooms with kids?

Madison touched his arm, bringing his attention back to the present. "You okay?" she whispered.

"I'm okay." He nodded toward the door. "I'm going to stay for a little bit. Why don't you head back and get some sleep. I'll grab a cab later."

Madison took his hand and stepped backward. She sat one of the chairs while she motioned for him to take the other. "I don't mind staying."

He was going to protest, and maybe it was a little selfish of him, but he liked the idea of her there with him. He took a seat and she leaned against him, resting her head on his shoulder. They both sat in silence, lost in their own thoughts, and after a while she asked, "Are you really going to move into the house?"

"No," he whispered.

"No?"

"I only said that to appease Granddad. I'm actually going to put it up for sale when I finish renovating."

There was a real sadness in her voice when she said, "That's too bad. I always loved visiting there with you and Jonah. It would have been nice to keep it in the family but Jonah told me he didn't want it, and I guess there's no reason for you to have a big old house like that."

"Why not?" he asked, his voice a little harsh, a little defensive. Even though he knew she was right, it felt like a kick in the teeth to hear her blatantly put it out there like that.

She gave an easy shrug, and her voice was sleepy when she said, "I mean you move around so much. In less than thirty days you'll be leaving again, and well..."

"Well, what?"

She lifted her head from his shoulder and looked at him. "A house like that kind of screams for a big family, don't you think?"

"Yeah, it does," he agreed, and then suddenly, catching him by surprise, the image of Madison in that house with him, filling it with kids, love and laughter, played out in his mind's eyes and damn near had him falling off his chair.

$$7$$

Madison flipped the sign on her bakery door from *Closed* to *Open* and stood there enjoying the beautiful, clear morning as warm rays of sunshine spilled over her body. She blinked the scratchiness from her eyes and ran her hand along her sore jaw. For the past few nights she'd been having the time of her life with Brad. After a long workday, they'd cook dinner together and then fall into bed. While she liked falling to sleep with him, she had to admit, waking up with him was just as nice. But the extended use of contacts and going without her bite plate was taking its toll. Not to mention the exhaustion she was fighting. It wasn't easy to sneak from the bed every morning so she could present Made-Up Madison to him when he woke up.

Brad stepped up behind her and pressed his chest to her back. Her body shivered in response when he put his mouth close to her ear and whispered, "You look gorgeous."

"I have a meeting." It was a half truth. She wanted to get dressed up for him, wanted to look like the kind of girl he normally dated, even though she wasn't all that comfortable in clothes that showcased her curves. She turned to face him and her heart pounded as she took in the man before her. Dressed in a pair of old, worn jeans and a work shirt, with a tool belt hanging low on his waist, he had to be the sexiest guy she'd ever met.

And for the rest of the month he is all mine.

That thought had a weird lump gathering in the pit of her stomach. Even though she liked Brad, *really* liked him—heck, who was she kidding, there was a good chance she was already half in love with him before they'd even begun this fling—she couldn't deny that one month would never be enough for her. But there was no way she could continue with this charade for more than that. Not without scratching her itchy eyeballs out and going on a diet of soft foods only. And of course, she couldn't forget that he was off relationships and had asked for one month only.

"I packed you a lunch," she said, talking quietly to keep her jaw from overworking.

He angled his head, and the look he gave her was genuinely appreciative, and so damn adorable her knees nearly gave out. "You didn't have to do that."

"If I didn't you'd end up working straight through lunch." She poked him in the chest. "I know you, Brad. You get so focused on a task you forget about everything else."

He laughed. "You didn't complain about that last night."

As her mind took that moment to reminisce about their bedroom play and the way he lost himself between her legs, she said, "That reminds me, I need to order more aprons."

At the mention of her apron, a growl crawled out of his throat. "Shit. You shouldn't have brought up the apron. Now all I can think of is tying you up in it again."

"Maybe later," she whispered, unable to believe how bold she'd become over the past few days. There was something about Brad that brought out the wicked in her.

"Oh yeah? How about tonight then?" he asked, a crooked grin on his face.

"Tonight, tomorrow night, and perhaps even the next," she teased. "After all, we still have more than three weeks left in this arrangement," she reminded him. A strange look came over his face, almost like he was waging an internal war. He seemed like he wanted to say something but instead just stood there, so she tapped his chest and said, "Then you'll be leaving on a convoy, Jonah will be moving back into his room, and my life will return to normal. Well, as normal as it can be while I'm still living in this old place."

Brad stiffened and inched back. At first she was confused by his reaction, but when she saw Sophie's car pulling into the parking lot she understood.

She gave him a little nudge and pointed to the door. "But right now you need to get to work on your granddad's place and I have a million cupcakes that need to be baked before tomorrow's festival."

He grabbed the door and the little bell overhead jangled as he pulled it open for Sophie. He mumbled something to her as he left the bakery, and both Madison and Sophie watched him walk to his truck.

After he drove off, Sophie frowned and turned to Madison.

"What?" Madison asked when she saw her friend crinkling her nose in worry.

"I don't know, Brad seemed kind of...I don't know put out or something?"

"Put out? Oh, don't worry, Sophie, he's still putting out."

Madison walked toward the counter, rearranging the chairs around the tables before she made her way to the back of the bakery to her baking area.

"No, I'm serious," Sophie said. "He looked a bit upset about something. What were you two talking about?"

Madison shrugged. "Just how we still had a little over three weeks together, and me living in this place."

"Maybe he's changed his mind?"

Unease moved through Madison. "Changed his mind?"

Sophie grabbed an apron and tied it around her waist as Madison pulled out all the cupcake trays from overhead storage. "Yeah, maybe he wants more." Her eyes lit up. "I knew it could happen."

Madison shook her head and reached for the flour, knowing better. "It's just sex."

Silence ensued for a long moment as Sophie's gaze moved over her face, accessing her. "Okay, if you say so. But I'm telling you. Something is going on with him."

Not wanting to talk about her sex life any longer, she nodded toward the fridge. "We better get a move on it. The bread needs to go in the oven before the breakfast crowd gets here."

Letting the subject drop, Sophie made her way to the fridge. As she retrieved the dough, Madison turned her attention to the daunting task before her. The morning passed rather quickly as Sophie served patrons and she baked, and once the lunch crowd died down, her friend clocked out for the day, needing to hit the books. In between serving the few people that strolled in after lunch, Madison continued to bake hundreds and hundreds of cupcakes. When the last of the patrons left, Madison turned the sign from *Open* to *Closed* and now stood back to examine her day's work.

Cupcakes lined her counters, but she wouldn't be able to put the icing on them until tomorrow morning, when they were thoroughly cooled. The band members wouldn't be stopping by to pick them up until noon so if she got up early, it would give her plenty of time to add the final touches. Then she and Brad could enjoy a few of the holiday festivities.

Brad...

As if thinking of him had suddenly conjured him up, she turned to find him behind her, looking like sex incarnate as he leaned against the wall. Her heart jumped as she swept her gaze down the length of him. Rough and rugged in his work wear, his jeans and shirt full of saw dust and debris, Brad was the epitome of sex, and her pussy responded accordingly.

"Hey," he said, stepping up to her.

Working to keep a modicum of composure, she smoothed her hair down with chipped nails full of batter, hating that he caught her in the kitchen looking like a hot mess.

"You're back a bit early."

"I brought dinner."

She smiled. "You did?"

As though not bothered by her disheveled state, he touched her shoulder, running his hands down her arm. "While it's been fun cooking together, I thought we could put our time to better use."

"Good idea," she said, feeling suddenly breathless as his thick muscles bunched. "We might as well take advantage of every minute while we still can." She glanced at the calendar on her wall and did the mental math on how many minutes they actually had.

Brad scrubbed his chin, a strange look on his face when she turned back to him, which had her thinking about what Sophie had said. Her skin prickled, but before she could ask if everything was okay, he gestured with a nod toward the microwave. "We'll have to reheat, because I need to get cleaned up first."

She looked at her soiled apron. "Me too."

Brad's hand went to her face. He brushed his thumb over her cheek, and a shiver skipped down her spine when he put it in his mouth. "Mmmm, chocolate."

Her eyes widened, mortified that she had food on her

face. She lifted her arm, but he stopped her. "Leave it. I'll clean it off in the shower." His grin turned wicked. "With my tongue."

He captured her hands in his and gave a little tug. She fell against him and he dropped a kiss onto her lips. His mouth moved urgently over hers, the heated kiss was so full of passion and need, her sex fluttered. The eagerness in his touch excited her and set her into motion.

"Come on," she said, desperate to feel him on top of her, inside her. She hurried toward the stairs and he kept pace behind her. Once they reached the landing, they stepped into the bathroom, and Brad headed straight for the shower. As he adjusted the spray, she shut the door, and when she turned back to face him, his body bumped hers.

His eyes darkened with want, and his fingers tangled through her hair as he backed her up against the closed door. A slow burn worked its way through her body, and her nipples grew taut.

"So about this chocolate," he said.

"What about it?" she asked as the bright bulbs over the vanity mirror bathed her body in artificial light, making her feel a bit self-conscious as Brad stared down at her.

"If I'm going to clean you with my tongue, I want to make sure I get every last spot." He ran his hands along her neck until he reached her cleavage. His fingers felt like fire on her skin as he lightly caressed her flesh. "Do you think you spilled any here?"

"It's quite possible," she said, feeling a little breathless from this sexy game he was playing, not to mention the hot steam filling the small room.

"Mmmm," he murmured, his hands trailing over her stomach. Her body convulsed, and an erotic whimper bubbled up from her throat. "What about here?" he asked, longing filling his voice as his warm breath fanned her face.

"There's...ah...there's a good chance." She reached around her back, untied the strings to her apron, and held it up. "This old thing doesn't catch everything."

His body trembled at the sight of her apron. Shaky hands dipped lower, until he reached the juncture between her legs. As he rubbed her sex through her pants, he asked, "What about here, sweetheart? Do you think you might need my tongue here?"

Her breath came fast. "I'm almost certain."

He cocked his head. "You're not one-hundred percent sure?"

"I'm pretty sure."

"Maybe I should check anyway."

"It's always better to be safe than sorry."

Steam swirled around them, and as it obscured their vision, she relaxed a bit. Even though Brad was completely comfortable in his skin, and had no trouble parading around naked, she preferred sex with the lights out. Up until now, she'd managed to make that happen through distraction. At least the hot steam prevented him from seeing her naked body this time around. She seriously doubted she could get away with turning the lights off and jumping into the shower with him without him becoming curious and questioning her. The last thing she wanted him to know was that she had body image issues. Talk about turning fantasy into reality.

His mouth grazed hers and he whispered. "I can barely see you." He drove a knee between her legs to widen them, then adjusted his stance. "I guess I'll just have to feel my way around."

She worked to find her voice. "You have a solution for everything don't you?"

He laughed. "Yeah, baby. When I want something bad enough, nothing stands in my way of getting it."

She inhaled his skin, loving the scent of him as she tugged

his T-shirt out from his worn jeans. He gripped it and pulled it over his shoulders, and even though she couldn't quite see him, a shiver tingled all the way to her toes as he stripped before her.

"Now you," he said.

Her hands went to the buttons on her blouse, and once she released them he pushed the fabric off her shoulders, his fingers lightly massaging her skin. He pulled the cups of her bra down and bent his head for a taste before unhooking the clasp in the back.

As her bra fell to the heap on the floor, she reached for his jeans, but his hands were already there, tearing them open like he couldn't get naked fast enough. She listened to the rustle of his clothes before they hit the floor with a thud.

"Your turn," he murmured. "And just so you know, you have three seconds to get naked or I'm going to rip the rest of your clothes off you."

"You wouldn't?" she asked, shocked by how much that idea excited her.

He stepped closer, and his voice dropped an octave when he said, "Try me."

Her entire body trembled. God, she loved this intense, take-charge side of him.

"One."

"Okay, okay." She laughed and she hurried out of her pants and panties. Once she was completely naked, he grabbed her waist and pulled her against him. His hard cock slapped against her stomach. No matter how many times she'd seen him aroused, it still shocked the hell out of her that she was the one arousing him.

He stepped over the edge of the tub, then helped her into the shower. As the hot spray spilled down her back he dipped his head for a kiss. He kissed her long and hard until they were both left shaking. After he pulled back, she gasped for air and his burning mouth went to her neck. He spent a long time running his tongue over the long column of her throat, and the moans coming from him told her how much he loved the taste of her skin.

His erection slapped against her stomach, and her mind filled with delicious ideas as her hands left his shoulders. She trailed them lower, running her palms over his chest until she reached his cock. His body stiffened when she took it into her hands.

As she enjoyed the feel of his hardness, she thought about the glorious nights they'd spent in bed, and how she'd yet to pleasure him orally. Brad had always taken the time to prepare her body, licking every inch of her, taking extra care not to miss a spot. But before she had the chance to return the favor, she always found him rolling on a condom, like he was too far gone to let her go down on him. Here in the shower, where no condoms could be found, she was going to do what she'd been aching to do for so long now. Her mouth watered just thinking about it.

"Oh, Jesus," he moaned when she squeezed her hand around his girth. His breath came hot on her neck and she turned sideways to aim the stream at his chest. Water spilled over his hard muscles, dripping down his erect cock. With one hand still on his erection, she grabbed the soap and lathered his chest. Once he was good and sudsy, she set the bar back down and put both slippery hands around his cock. His hips jerked, his cock easily sliding in and out of her slick palms. She stroked him gently, enjoying the feel of him in her hands as his body trembled. With need erupting inside her, she gripped the shower nozzle and directed it toward his cock. His muscles bunched as water splashed against him and she could hear his impatient curses, sense the urgency building in him. Once the water washed the last remnants of soap away, she grabbed him by the waist and turned him until the stream was on his back.

Just as she was about to slide down his body, his warm, work-roughened palms gently cupped her cheeks to stop her. While she couldn't see his face in the steamy shower, she could hear surprise creeping into his voice when he asked, "What are you doing, baby?"

"Something I've wanted to do for a long time," she murmured, her heart pounding erratically against her chest as she thought about tasting him. Taking charge of their play, she pulled away from his tenuous hold, and dropped to her knees.

Brad's moan filled the small space as she leaned forward to draw him into her mouth, taking him as deeply as possible. She cupped his balls, massaging them in her palm until they grew tight.

"Fuck," he growled, his fingers fisting her hair as pure satisfaction flowed through her.

Her body burned and her pussy ached to feel his hardness inside her as his cock swelled even more. She began rocking into him, his hands holding her head and following the motion. His breathing changed, and she could feel his blood rushing fast, filling the veins in his cock. She ran her tongue over his crown, moaning when she tasted the juices dripping from his slit.

When she whimpered in delight, he gripped her head harder, his body tightening with the tension of an impending orgasm. A wave of passion overcame her, loving that she could do this to him, loving that she could make him feel this good. She gripped him with her palms, forming a tight channel. He thrust forward, pushing in and out of her grip, the tip of his cock meeting her mouth on the other end.

Air rushed from his lungs and he began panting as she slid her tongue over him. "It's good. Jesus, it's so good, baby."

She gave a throaty purr and licked him as more pre-come dripped from his slit. "I love the taste of you," she said.

"Oh, fuck, Madison. I'm right there." His voice sounded rough as he tried to pull her head away.

Staying deep between his legs, she wrapped her lips around him and sucked hard, wanting him to release in her mouth. His cock swelled, and he held her head still as a moan crawled out of his throat. She cupped his balls again, and a second later he growled, his hips jerking forward as he gave himself over to the pleasure. He released hard and as she drank him in, his hands went to her face again. He gently brushed his thumbs over her cheeks, and her heart hitched, understanding that what she'd just done had somehow created a deeper intimacy between them. Unable to ignore the sudden barrage of emotions careening through her, she closed her eyes, and worked to get herself under control. When his cock stopped pulsing, she inched back, unable to believe how emotionally close she felt to him.

"Hey," Brad said and grabbed her shoulders to tug her to her feet. "Come here," he murmured quietly.

She stood and he pulled her close, locking his arms around her waist. As she listened to his heart pound, she melted against him, loving this new, easy intimacy between them. As her emotions began to get the better of her, she worked to keep them in check, and to concentrate only on the physical things he made her feel.

Brad stayed quiet, too quiet. With his face buried in her hair, he continued to hold her, a little too tight, his breathing still labored, unsteady.

Suddenly getting the sense that something was wrong, unease cramped her stomach. "Brad?" she asked, her voice a hesitant whisper.

After a long moment he said, "Yeah?"

"Are you okay?"

"I'm okay."

"Are you sure?"

She inched back, desperate to see his eyes through the steam, but he grabbed her and pulled her to him, burying his face in her wet hair. "Why did you do that?" he asked, and her pulse leapt, astonished by the tenderness in his tone.

"I wanted to." Even though it was a ridiculous thing to ask, considering the powerful orgasm he just had, she asked it anyways. "Didn't you like it?"

A tortured noise sounded in his throat. "I liked it, baby. I liked it a lot." He exhaled slowly. "It's just...well...you don't have to do that for me."

Sensing there was more going on than he was saying, and that it likely had everything to do with his ex and the number she'd done on him, she attempted to lighten the mood. She wiggled against him, sandwiching his still-hard cock between their bodies and whispered, "Did you ever think that maybe I wanted to?"

He ran his hands over her back, touching her in such a familiar way, a way she loved so much. A shudder moved through her as her breasts rubbed up against his chest. "Yeah," he breathed into her mouth as one hand slipped between her thighs to urge them apart. "Well, there are some things that I want to do to you too."

Her pulse leapt, her pussy moistened, but before she could answer, to tell him just how much she'd like that, the water turned cold. She yelped, and Brad backed her up and out of the spray. He turned to shut the water off, but when a loud clang sounded, and they could hear water rushing in the walls, he said, "Oh, shit."

"What happened?"

"I think something just broke."

"Oh no." Madison pulled back the shower curtain, grabbed two towels, and opened the bathroom door to clear the steam. She covered herself as Brad took his towel and wrapped it around his waist.

He rushed from the bathroom and she listened to his footstep on the stairs as she made her way to her bedroom. Pipes clanged as he shut off the water, and her stomach knotted, knowing she had to find a better place to live sooner rather than later. She pulled on a pair of jeans and a T-shirt, padding barefoot down the hall to find him.

Brad hurried up the stairs and when she saw the look on his face, she stilled and asked, "What?"

"The good news is I found the problem and I can fix it."

"And the bad news?" she asked, taking in his troubled expression.

"Your cupcakes, most of them are ruined. The pipe that broke was above your kitchen and water leaked through the ceiling and onto your counter." Madison wrapped her arms around herself, and Brad pushed her hair off her face. "It's not so bad. It could be a lot worse. And hey, we can always make more."

"Not without water, I can't."

He frowned. "Yeah, you're right."

"I really don't want to let those kids down." As she worried her bottom lip, his fingers closed over hers, a great deal of tenderness on his face. "They're counting on my donation."

"I tell you what." He turned her around and slapped her ass to set her into motion. "Go pack a bag, then meet me in the kitchen. We'll gather up what we need and take them to Granddad's old place."

"Granddad's place?"

"Sure. If Grandma could bake dozens of pies in that kitchen every Sunday, then surely we can bake hundreds of cupcakes overnight, right?"

"Are you serious?"

"Yeah, why not?"

She shrugged, unable to come up with a reason why they couldn't. Her heart swelled as she looked at Brad, thankful that he was there with her, for so many reasons. "You really do have a solution for everything."

"Yeah, now come on. It's still early, and if we work through the night, we can get it done."

"You're going to help me?"

"Of course." He flashed a devious smile. "But on one condition."

In spite of the situation she laughed and arched a curious brow. "You have a condition?"

His grin broadened. "Yeah, no aprons."

8

Brad took one look at the woman moving around his late grandmother's kitchen and his heart swelled almost painfully. Soft music drifted from the old radio perched on top of the refrigerator as Madison hummed softly and mixed a huge bowl full of batter.

A tremor raced through him as he stirred sugar into his coffee and stirred it with a spoon. He tried to focus on the task she'd given him, he really did, but how could he be expected to concentrate when she was swaying her hips, her long silken hair tumbling down her back in erotic ways. As his fingers itched to grab a fistful of her curls, all he could think about was dragging her upstairs and finishing what they started in the shower.

As he continued to watch her, his mind recalled his last conversation with his granddad. Surely to God it was the dementia talking right? He wasn't the *boy* Madison always wanted. If he were, wouldn't he have known? Of course there was a chance his Granddad was right and he really was dense.

She tested the batter, poured a handful of chocolate chips into the bowl and went back to stirring. Brad took a sip of his coffee and let his glance fall over the sexy woman he'd been falling into bed with every night. Seeing her happy and relaxed as she baked, completely in her element in the big old kitchen, had him thinking about how envious he was of his friends who were either married or getting married. Truthfully, he was glad he found out who his ex was before he walked that path, but he had to admit, there were times when loneliness nipped at his soul.

Madison wiped her hands on the towel masquerading as an apron, and her movements drew his focus. As she left streaks of chocolate on the towel, one that, unfortunately, hindered his view and prevented him from ogling her ass in those curve-hugging jeans, he took a moment to consider her clothing. It was odd that she wasn't in her baggy work wear—ones that hid her femininity—with her hair tied back and glasses on, the way she always used to dress when in the kitchen. Even though he found it strange, he suddenly became too preoccupied with the easy way she was moving about the kitchen, like it was where she was always meant to be, to give her clothing any more thought.

As he continued to watch her, he thought more about his failed relationship. He couldn't deny that he missed being with someone, and watching Madison fill pans with batter while humming happily to herself gave him a sample of what life would be like with her living in this house.

With him.

Oh, Jesus. This was just sex, he quickly reminded himself. He was on the road all the time and knew from past experiences that long-distance relationships never worked, which meant he was not going to walk that path again and set himself up for heartache. Not that he thought Madison really was interested in more, anyway. Lord knows she reminded him enough that there was an expiration date on this fling.

Then again, he was the one who'd set the terms. She was just happy to abide by them.

"Brad?" she began, wiping the flour from her face with the back of her hand before she reached for another cupcake pan. "Can you set the timer for me?" she asked again.

Seeing those streaks of chocolate on her face had him reminiscing about the shower again, and the way she'd taken him into her mouth. He shifted, his cock aching to feel her lips wrapped around him again.

"Brad?"

"Right, right, the timer." He cleared his throat to pull himself together.

She shot him a glance. "Actually, what I was going to ask is what's so funny?"

"Funny?"

"Yeah, you're smiling."

"I am."

"Yeah. Why?"

"Because of you," he answered, pushing off the counter.

"Me?" she asked as she licked batter from the spatula before tossing it into the sink. "What did I do?"

As he thought about how much he enjoyed being around her, how cute she looked with batter on her face, he asked, "What is it with you and chocolate, anyway?" He wiped her cheek with his thumb, and heat moved over her face, as if she too was thinking back to what they'd done earlier that night.

She arched a challenging brow, and beneath the exhaustion in her eyes he could see the heat. "You got something against chocolate?"

"Not when it's smeared over your body, I don't."

His hands skimmed her contours and he brushed his lips over hers. "Mmmm, delicious," he murmured, then stuck his finger in the batter to swipe more across her mouth. He kissed it off as he thought about smearing the rest over her entire body and cleaning it off with his tongue. As he visualized that sexy scenario, it occurred to him that they'd been sleeping together for a few nights now, and he'd yet to really see her. That gave him pause, but before he could give it any further consideration, Madison stifled a yawned.

His heart twisted when he noted the time. He glanced out the window to see the sun cresting the horizon. As a soldier who worked in the field, Brad was used to going without sleep but he knew Madison needed her rest, especially after just getting over a cold. Licking chocolate from her body would have to wait.

"Is this the last batch?" he asked.

"Yes, but then I have to wait until they're cooled before I can decorate."

"Why don't you go on up and get some sleep. I'll stay up until this batch is done, then I'll join you."

"You don't have to do that." She pushed her hair from her face, but her eyes looked tired when she said, "These cupcakes are my responsibility."

He tucked a long strand of hair behind her ear. "It's a nice thing you're doing for those kids."

She went quiet, thoughtful for a moment. "It's important to them, which makes it important to me."

"Band geeks do stick together," he teased.

"Hey." She whacked him. "Be nice."

He feigned hurt, but moved closer, until his lips were hovering over hers. "I'm always nice, and did you forget that I was also in the band, which makes the cause important to me too."

"You played the drums in the senior band, which hardly made you a geek." She poked him in the chest. "And what I remember, from my lowly spot in the junior band, is that all the girls were after you."

"You weren't," he said, his eyes moving over her as he thought about what granddad had said.

"You were a senior. I was a junior."

"And?"

"The two don't mix."

"We're mixing now."

Her eyes dimmed with desire as his mouth moved closer to hers, but underneath the lust he could see exhaustion pulling at her. "And as much as I'd like to mix it up some more," he murmured as he lightly brushed his mouth over hers, "you need sleep. So go on and get upstairs and let me take care of this."

"You really don't have to," she whispered, her throat working as she swallowed.

He cocked his head. "Maybe I want to, Madison." Before she could protest, he slipped the towel from around her waist, and gave her a tap on the ass to set her into motion. "Take the room on the left at the top of the stairs."

"Your old room?"

"Yeah. Go get a few hours of sleep. You can't really do much until these cool."

She ran her hands through her hair again, and looked a little unsure. "What about you?"

"I just had coffee, so I'm going to be up for a while anyway." He turned her and faced her toward the hall. "Now go on. I'll be up soon."

"Okay," she said, and as he watched her go, his gaze dropping to the sexy swell of her ass, he once again wondered about her work wear. Wouldn't she have been more comfortable baking all night in those sweats of hers, ones that set his imagination on fire?

As he mulled that over, he finished the last of his coffee, reset the timer and strolled through the house, running his hands along the antique furniture that he'd be selling with the place. He thought more about Madison as he walked around the room, looking at the few repairs that still needed to be done before he put the place up for sale. Unlike the old rundown building Madison and his brother lived in, this was a good sturdy home with good bones. It would provide well for a growing family and was in a sought-after district, with great schools.

He looked at the old swing in the tree out back and couldn't help but smile. How many times had Jonah wrapped himself around the tree, only to end up calling Brad to his rescue? Granddad was right; the boy really was a fool sometimes. Could he have been right about Madison too?

Brad continued through the house, until the timer went off. Hurrying back to the kitchen, he pulled the cupcakes from the oven and shook them from the tray. He stifled a yawn and set them on the cooling rack.

He knew he should probably get a few hours of sleep himself. After all, he'd promised Jack he'd help out at the festival, showcasing the dogs they were training. He walked along the shiny wood floor he'd recently refinished and climbed the set of stairs leading to the bedroom he'd used when sleeping over at his grandparents. He inched the door open quietly, not wanting to wake Madison. But when he caught her sprawled across his bed, her long hair a tangled mess, her jeans and shirt neatly folded on the rocking chair, lust hit like a high voltage jolt and his body urged him to wake her.

To take her.

It was warm in the room. Not only from the baking, but from the early morning sun shining in through the lace curtains his grandma had made. At some point in her sleep Madison had kicked the blankets to the foot of the bed, giving him his first up close and personal view of her beautiful body. He let his glance leisurely trail over her near nakedness, taking his time to look at her, *really* look at her. He took plea-sure in the creamy softness of her skin as well as the lush curves in her body. Most women from his circle dieted down to skin and bone, and he had to admit, he loved Madison's full figure.

He took a step closer, and the old floorboards creaked under his weight. She shifted, rolling onto her side. He stilled until she settled back down. With her legs pulled to her chest, she looked so peaceful, so at home in his old bed. Once again, catching him off guard, he couldn't help but imagine what life would be like with her living in this big place.

He pulled his shirt over his shoulders and kicked off his boots, but when he approached the bed, her lids flicked open.

"Brad?" she murmured, blinking up at him.

"Yeah, it's me. Go back to sleep, we still have a few hours."

Her glance went to the window, and she squinted against the bright light. "How long have I been asleep?"

"Not long," he said, sitting on the mattress beside her. "Close your eyes and try to get a couple more hours, okay?"

"The cupcakes?"

"They're cooling." He brushed her hair from her face and breathed in her warm scent. Jesus, the depth of desire he felt for her was beyond his comprehension.

Suddenly her eyes went wide, and she scrambled to reach the blankets at the foot of the bed. Despite the heat in the room, she grabbed the sheets and pulled them up to her neck, a stricken look on her face.

"Hey." He smoothed her hair back. "What's wrong?"

"Nothing," she said, her voice deceptively calm. "It's just cold."

Cold? It was a million degrees in the room.

As he looked at her, he thought more about how they always made love with the lights out, and that's when it suddenly occurred to him that she'd been purposely hiding her body from him. What the hell? He's been inside her, for Christ's sake, and now, without the cover of darkness, she was going to go all shy on him.

"Madison?" he said, his throat feeling tight.

"Yeah?" she asked as he toyed with the bed sheet, running the soft material between his thumb and index finger and he ever so slowly pulled it away from her neck.

"I want to see you."

She gulped. "You can see me."

"No," he said, daring to pull the sheet lower, until it reached the soft, creamy swell of her breasts. "I really want to see you. All of you."

Her body stiffened and when she looked like she was about to flee, he put his hand on her stomach, trapping her on the bed.

"Brad," she whispered, and even though her voice was shaky, something resembling lust moved over her face, and the way her long lashes were fluttering told him just how much she liked it when he took charge.

"Do you have any idea how beautiful your body is?" He exposed her bra, and his nostrils flared when he saw the tightening of her nipples beneath the lace material. He wet his mouth and ran his thumb over her hard buds. "Don't you see, sweetheart? I don't want to just feel these swell in my mouth, I want to see them."

Heat flared between them and despite the color creeping up her neck, passion grew in her eyes. Using unhurried movements, he dragged the sheets to her waist. He ran his hands over her silky soft stomach, and moved his palms to her sides to shape the sweeping curves of her lush contours.

Jesus, she was so fucking sexy.

She sucked in a breath, and when he felt her shying away, he said, "You are the most beautiful woman I've ever set eyes on." Her lashes lowered, shadowing her emotions. "Look at me."

She blinked up at him, and as their gazes connected and locked, her fingers curled in the bed sheets beneath her. He moaned with pleasure as he slowly bared her body to him. Even though there was a hit of anxiety in her gaze, she didn't stop him when he continued with his downward exploration.

He skimmed her flesh, taking note of the goose bumps, and when she went perfectly still, he teased, "You should try to breathe, sweetheart."

Her chest heaved as she filled her lungs, her eyes never leaving his as he exposed the white lace on her panties. The scent of her arousal permeated the room and urged him on. Continuing to push her past her comfort zone, and refusing to let her hide herself from him, he pressed on, lowering the sheets until they pooled at her feet. Her legs clamped together, but he wasn't about to have any of that.

Once he had her exposed, heat moved through his blood and his body began pulsing with need. He ran his fingers along her thighs as electricity sizzled between them. When his throat dried all he could think about was spreading her wide, burying his face in her sweet pussy and quenching his thirst with her cream. As she writhed beneath his touch, he vowed to never—ever—make love to her in the dark again.

"A body this beautiful should never be covered," he murmured, bending forward to press a kiss to her pelvis. He brushed his tongue over her tightening flesh and moaned.

As a tremble moved through her, he acknowledged the flare of desire in her eyes, noted the telltale hardening of her nipples.

"Brad," she murmured.

He looked up at her, and physically felt the shiver that stole over her. He held her body to absorb it and said, "Yeah."

"I just...I'm not..."

He pitched his voice low. "You don't have to be shy, sweetheart. Not with me."

"But I don't..."

Intent on giving her a little incentive to help her relax, he slipped a finger inside her panties, and swiped her clit. Her words fell off and her hips came off the bed, a whimper sounding deep in her throat.

"I want to see your pussy, baby. I want to see how wet you are."

Without giving her time to think, and wanting her to get out of her head and just enjoy the pleasure, he gripped the band on her panties, and gave a little tug. He dragged the scrap of material down her legs, until they reached her mid-thigh. When he saw the damp hairs on her perfectly groomed pussy, his body rippled. While he wanted to dive in and stay there for the rest of the day, his first goal was to help her loosen up, to get used to him looking at her body. Because now that he'd unveiled it, he planned on looking at it. A lot.

He widened her sex with his finger and gulped air when he glimpsed her wet pinkness. "Ah Jesus," he bit out, scrubbing his other hand through his hair as he tried to keep his shit together. "So fucking pretty."

"Oh God," she whispered, going up on her elbows and squeezing her thighs tighter together as he better positioned himself of the bed.

He stroked her. "Don't you want to show me your pussy?

"I just..."

"You do want my mouth on you, don't you, baby?" As he mentally indulged in the slideshow, he filled his lungs with her scent and asked, "You do want me to lick you and put my fingers inside, right?"

She nodded.

"Say it."

"I want you to lick my pussy."

"And?"

"And I want your fingers inside me."

In a voice that was commanding yet soft, he said, "Then open your legs."

She wet her mouth and sank back onto the pillow as she slowly inched her legs open.

"Wider," he demanded as chaos erupted inside him. "And look at me." When smoldering eyes met his, he drew a breath and worked to calm his cock. She was so incredibly beautiful and the way she was softening, offering herself up so nicely to him, took his breath away.

Even though he wanted to pound into her, hot ramming strokes that would leave them both breathless, he first needed to lavish her gorgeous body with attention.

"Brad," she croaked out, and while he could still sense a bit of unease, the excitement on her face was all the encouragement he needed.

His eyes left hers and the second he glimpsed her hot pussy, moisture glistening in the early morning rays, he said, "A pussy this hot and needy should never be hidden." He stroked her gently. "In fact, now that I've seen it, I don't ever want it covered in panties again."

"Ever?" she croaked out.

"Ever."

"You...you want me to go three weeks without panties?"

He bit down on his cheek, hating her constant reminder of their timeline, but right now he wasn't going to dwell on that. Right now he had a hot wet pussy in desperate need of attention, and the only thing he wanted to think about was bringing her to orgasm with his mouth, his fingers and his cock.

As he ran the rough pad of his thumb around her clit, he leaned forward to draw her beautiful dark nipple into his mouth. He moaned and sucked hard. She arched into him, her hands going to her stomach.

"Put your hands over your head," he commanded around one delicious nipple.

She quivered beneath him. "What?" she whimpered.

He lightly bit her hard nub and when she squealed he lifted his head. "I want your hands over your head." He jutted his chin toward the slats in the headboard. "Grab on to those and keep your hands there. That way I can see your entire body."

"Oh. My. God," she murmured, but did as he said.

Once she gripped the wooden slats, he inched back and let his gaze fall over her. His gut tightened with the way she trusted him with her body, her hands over her head and her legs spread wide. His heart pinched and in that instant pleasuring her became more important than his next breath.

As he gifted himself with one more minute of gazing, an erotic whimper bubbled in her throat, but he continued to stare, taking his sweet time to drink in every inch of her nakedness even though he could barely wait to feel skin against skin.

She squirmed, her big breasts jiggling, beckoning his mouth. Her pleasure resonated through him as he dipped his head. He licked her, and as he stimulated her nipples, she liquefied under his touch.

"That's it, baby." He turned his attention to her other breast and, as he lavished her with attention, he murmured. "Just feel, don't think."

He could sense the nervous tension easing from her body, desire moving in to take its place as he ran the tip of his tongue around her areola. Suddenly impatient to hold her, kiss her, make love to her, he climbed from the bed and tore off his pants. Her eyes widened and ecstasy flitted across her face as she stared at his throbbing hard-on. Jesus he loved the way she looked at him, desired him.

Desperate to be inside her and wanting her to lose herself in him—the same way he was losing himself in her—he climbed between her legs and buried his mouth in her sweet pussy. Her hips came off the bed, her body a trembling mess as he increased the pressure, needing, in the most inexplicable way, to make her come for him. As his internal temperature spiked, desire clouding his brain, he worked to slow down, but he couldn't seem to help himself. There was a deep ache in his core that he couldn't seem to alleviate. Pushing two fingers inside her, he caressed her sensitive bundle of nerves, his cock anxious to reacquaint itself with her hot channel.

"So good," she cried out, her hips moving, coming off the bed as he stroked her deep.

Need gathered in his core as he fucked her with his fingers, her body rippling beneath him. She cried out his name and once he felt her release, her hot cream dripping over his hand, he rolled on a condom and gripped her hips.

"I need to be inside you," he rushed out as he dropped to the bed and lifted her onto him.

As she straddled him, a warm flush on her cheeks, he gripped her hips and lowered her onto his hard cock. Her pussy was so damp with passion, he easily slid into her. A moan caught in her throat, the sweet sound urging him on. He powered into her and her head rolled back as he filled her completely.

"Baby," he cried as he ravaged her drippy pussy. He dragged her down onto him, then lifted her again. When her breath caught, he slowed only long enough for her to catch it again, then continued to pound into her with hot hard strokes, unable to get enough of her.

He swelled inside her tight sheath, and as he took her

breasts into his hands, her palms skimmed his muscles. His body quaked, loving the way she touched him, the way she wanted him.

Teetering on the edge of ecstasy, and completely lost in the sensation, he began trembling and panting, knowing he wasn't going to last long. His breath came in a low rush as one hand left her breast to rub her clit. The second his finger connected with her engorged nub, she screamed out his name.

When she clenched around his cock, every muscle in his body tightened. "Fuck," he cried out, her hot cream scorching him in mind-fucking ways.

As she came apart, her legs tightened around his, and her pussy muscles squeezed his dick. The onslaught of pleasure damn near killed him, but the desire reflecting in her eyes became his undoing. His skin grew tight and his balls constricted. Flames surged inside him and he took a deep breath, but he was well past the point of no return. He grabbed her waist, his fingers pressing into her soft flesh hard enough to leave a bruise as he let go, depleting himself inside her.

She leaned forward, falling over him. Her heart pounded against his rib cage as they both rode out the pleasure. After a long time, she slid off his body. He flinched as his cock slipped out of her and he instantly missed her warmth.

He disposed of the condom quickly, then drew her to him. As he held her tight and thought about the way she opened for him, he ran his fingers up and down her arm, leaving the blankets at the foot of the bed so he could continue to look at her. He angled his body, put his finger under her chin and tipped her face to his.

"Just so you know," he said, a wave of deep satisfaction moving through him as his gaze met hers. "We're never having sex with the lights out again."

9

At the far end of the football field in the center of town, where the afternoon Fourth of July festivities were taking place, Brad worked with his buddy Jack to set up obstacles for the upcoming dog show. What he'd hoped to avoid, however, was the onslaught of questions regarding his relationship with Madison. Except this was Jack he was with, which meant an interrogation was unavoidable.

"So you're just friends, then?" Jack asked.

Brad gave a casual roll of his shoulder and swiped his forehead as the hot afternoon sun beat down on them. "I told you, I'm staying with her and helping repair her plumbing problems while Jonah is away."

Jack adjusted his ball cap and arched a questioning brow. "Jonah doesn't mind?"

"Jonah is the one who asked me to take care of her and help her around the place."

"And you're sure Jonah and Madison aren't..." He paused and waved his hand. "Well, you know."

Brad gave a quick shake of his head. "I'm sure. They're just friends. That's all they've ever been."

"Glad to hear it," Jack said as he grabbed a canine training box from the back of his pickup truck.

"Oh yeah, why?" Brad shut the tail gate behind him and leaned against it.

Jack placed the last box on top of the others, straightened to his full height, and stood face to face with Brad. "Because if Madison and Jonah *were* a couple, then you know I'd have no choice but to kick your ass for sleeping with your brother's girl, right?"

As the word *sleeping* hovered around them, the meaning behind it loud and clear, Brad blew a breath, knowing he could never ever hide anything from Jack. The man was too smart, and too nosey, for his own damn good.

"For the record, I'd never sleep with another man's girl." Turning the focus to Jack, he said, "I thought you knew me better than that."

Jack nodded and looked contemplative for a moment as he stared at the ground, like he was remembering the shit storm Brad had gone through with Jocelyn. Jack, as well as the rest of Brad's comrades, knew full well how Brad felt about monogamy in committed relationships.

After a moment, he looked Brad square in the eyes again and asked, "So you are sleeping with her, then?"

Brad threw his hands up in the air, wanting to put an end to this conversation. "Okay fine, so we're sleeping together. Big fucking deal."

Jack held his hands up, palms out. "Hey, I never said it was a big deal."

"Well, it's not a big deal. It's just sex." Brad sidestepped Jack to place detonation material into the plywood detection wall they used for training. "When Jonah gets back, I'm leaving on a convoy, and Madison and I will be calling it quits." He turned back around to find Jack glaring at him and before he could stop himself he blurted out, "It's just sex."

"Okay, I get it, it's just sex. You said that already."

Feeling more defensive by the minute, Bran continued, "Look we're both grown adults. We can do what we want. If we want to have sex for a month, then we'll have sex for a month. I don't know what your fucking problem is with it."

Jack eyed him, a shit-eating grin on his face. "I'm not sure I'm the one who has a problem with it."

"Good, then, can we talk about something else."

"Like what? The real reason you set a deadline for this thing between you two?"

"Look—"

The smile fell from Jack's face. "She's not Jocelyn, you know."

Brad stiffened. "What's that supposed to mean?"

Jack shrugged. "Nothing."

"Nothing?"

"What it means," Cole said, coming up behind them, "is that Jack here doesn't know how to mind his own business." He turned to Jack and cocked his head. "Isn't that right, Jack?"

Jack greeted Cole with a nod. "Cole, I'm glad you're here. I've been meaning to tell you something."

"What's that?"

Jack grinned. "Go fuck yourself."

With that Cole laughed and turned to Brad. "So what's this I hear about you and Madison having sex for one month?"

"Jesus Christ," Brad groaned. "You're like a bunch of fucking women." He looked past Cole's shoulder to see Josh Mansfield jogging down the field toward them, five training dogs running beside him. The spectator stands near their end of the field began to fill up, viewers taking their seats in preparation for the upcoming show, one that would hopefully increase public awareness and gain more funding for Gemma's no-kill shelter and their cause.

Bandit, one of the dogs Brad had grown fond of, came sauntering over, a tennis ball in his mouth. "Hey, boy." Brad bent to scrub him behind the ears, happy for the distraction. "You going to help me put on a show today?" He pulled the ball from Bandit's mouth and tossed it down the field. As he watched the dog run after it, he spotted Madison standing by the band booth, looking over the table filled with the cupcakes they'd spent all night baking.

His heart tightened in his chest and breathing became difficult as he watched her. She flipped her hair from her shoulders and gesticulated with her hands as she talked to the kids and helped them sell her goods. Christ, the woman never stopped giving.

Jack was right. Madison wasn't Jocelyn. Jocelyn never would have stayed up all night and baked for the band, donating what little time and money she had for a cause that didn't benefit her.

Suddenly, as if she sensed him looking at her, Madison angled her head. When their eyes met and locked and they exchanged a long, heated look, his body reacted, thinking about all the ways he'd taken her earlier that morning. Thinking about how she was pantiless beneath that sexy sundress covering her curvy body.

His cock hardened, and a groan crawled out of his throat. Bandit came back with the ball, but Brad had no fucking idea how he was going to stand without his comrades seeing his hard-on. Fuck, the last thing he wanted to do was answer more questions or stand there while they razzed the shit out of him. He cursed under his breath and stayed crouched low as he tossed the ball again.

When Sophie stepped up to Madison, Madison turned her attention to her friend. They spoke for a moment, then

Karley and her newborn baby, Brooklyn, who were staying with Sophie until her husband returned from overseas, joined them. The women talked for a moment and Madison came out from behind the table. They slowly walked toward his end of the field. From his distance he couldn't tell what they were saying, but from the way Sophie was aiming her gaze his way, he knew it had to be about him. A moment later, Gemma joined the trio, and as she rubbed her stomach it reminded him of her upcoming baby shower. He groaned, hating the idea of going, but knowing he would just the same.

As he thought about Gemma's invitation to Madison, he considered asking her to come along, but then changed his mind, remembering how she wasn't all that comfortable with Jack's latest girlfriend. In fact, it pissed him off to think that Madison had been picked on and teased back in the day. Then another thought hit. Maybe her shyness with him went deeper. Maybe she was still harboring insecurities from her high school days. Jesus, did she not see what he saw, feel what he felt when he looked and touched her gorgeous body?

Before he could give that any more thought, someone stepped up to him. Shading the sun from his eyes, he glanced up, but from the strappy high heels, to the familiar scent of her perfumed skin, he didn't need to see her face to know who was invading his space, physical and mental.

Brad's eyes moved up and over skin-tight designer jeans that showcased long slim legs to a body-hugging tank top that highlighted a trim body and creamy white cleavage. He lifted his head higher, and when he came face to face with none other than his ex, his desire dissolved and he bit down on his teeth hard enough to grind bone. He cleared his throat and climbed to his feet, taking one distancing step back.

"Brad!" Jocelyn flashed a brilliant smile and fluttered those long lashes at him in a way that always melted his resolve and had him caving to her wants. Which begged the question, what did she want from him this time?

"I haven't seen you around," she said, her voice bright and cheery, but underneath her light tone he heard something else, something that sounded like regret and loneliness.

He caught Cole's questioning glance and signaled with a tight nod. Cole returned the nod, but stayed within earshot. "I've been around," Brad responded, the mere sight of her bringing back old hurts.

"I drove by your granddad's place but you weren't there."

"I'm not staying there."

Her eyes widened. "Where are you staying?"

Without conscious thought, he looked past Jocelyn's shoulders and when he saw Madison staring at him, watching the exchange with his ex, he once again found himself comparing the two. Jocelyn angled her head and followed his gaze.

"Oh," she said, pointing one manicured finger in Madison's direction. "Are you staying with Jonah and Madison?"

"Something like that."

Jocelyn narrowed those big blue eyes of hers and Brad could practically hear the wheels spinning. As he watched her, his stomach tightened. There was a time, not that long ago, that he loved her, a time when things were good. But she'd changed, couldn't handle him being away, despite the fact that he was off fighting a war to protect her and their country.

After a moment of silence, Brad shoved his hands in his pocket, and asked, "What can I do for you, Jocelyn?"

"You still have some things at my place." She stepped closer, too close, and put her hand on his chest. She curled her fingers in his shirt in a familiar way, bringing back so many memories, good ones and bad. "Why don't you come by and pick them up."

"If I've gone without them this long, then I'm pretty sure I don't need them."

"Come on, Brad," she cooed, puckering those painted lips in a way that always turned him inside out. "You're not still mad at me, are you?"

"Look, Jocelyn." He closed his hand over hers to remove it from his chest. "I don't want to do this." He looked around to see many sets of eyes on them. "Not here. Not with so many people watching."

"Then come by my place," she whispered her voice full of promise. "I'll make us dinner and we'll...talk."

"We don't have anything to talk about," he said, even though the look in her eyes told him talking was the last thing she had in mind. "Conversation between us ended when you wrapped your mouth around another man's cock."

Shock moved over her eyes, but then her face softened. Changing tactics, she went up on her tiptoes, and put her mouth close to his ear, making it look to all the world like they were still lovers. "He's no longer in my life and I'd like to make things up to you. If you know what I mean."

Before he could answer, Bandit came rushing back to him. Still not the most disciplined dog in the bunch, he nudged the saliva-coated ball toward Jocelyn.

She jumped back and her eyes sparked anger. "Eww, that's disgusting. Get him away from me."

"Here, boy," Brad said, dropping to one knee to pat him. Cole released Skid, the German Shepherd he'd been playing tug-of-war with, sending him Brad's way.

Jocelyn took another distancing step back as the Shepherd dashed toward him and skidded to a stop, hence his name.

"So I'll see you soon, then?" she asked.

"I don't—"

"I'll see you soon, Brad," she said firmly, the spark in her eyes worrying him.

He was about to protest, but she twisted in her heels and disappeared into the crowd. Brad blew an exaggerated breath and turned toward Jack.

"Everything okay?"

"Fine," he said, much harsher than he intended. He shook his head to clear it, and when Bandit sat down next to him and whined, clearly sensing his distress, he scrubbed the dog's head. "Come on, Bandit. Let's show the crowd what you can do."

Brad's comrades and their canines spent the next forty-five minutes entertaining the crowd. Brad and Bandit stepped in for the finale. He snapped on the dog's leash and put his thumb over the trigger in his pocket. He guided Bandit along the detection wall, pointing to each opening in the wood. When Bandit found the box containing the explosive evidence, he barked, and sat on the ground, his tail wagging wildly. As the crowd watched on, delight written all over their faces, Brad squeezed the trigger and a tennis ball went flying across the field. He let go of Bandit's leash and the dog went running after it.

His demonstration was met with a standing ovation and when the cheers died down, the guys all walked their dogs in front of the crowd. Once the show was over, he checked his watch, deciding he still had time to take Bandit, who was also used as a therapy dog, to Granddad's nursing home.

He spoke to the guys for a few minutes, then with Bandit in tow, went in search of Madison to let her know where he was going. Not that he needed to inform her. After all, they weren't in a committed relationship where they shared everything. But oddly enough he found himself wanting to tell her, because he liked the idea of them always knowing where the other one was. His heart beat a little faster in his chest when he found her in the stands with her friend, her back to him.

"Hey," he said, coming up behind her.

She turned quickly, and when she stumbled slightly on the metal stand, her shin hitting the step below her, he wrapped his arm around her waist. Lifting her clear off the steps, he pulled her tight against him and lowered her to the ground. When her breasts crushed against his chest and a slight breeze blew over their bodies, ruffling the material on her dress, his hand slid to the small of her back. Right to where the top of her panties would rest, had she been wearing any. His nostrils flared and he worked to marshal his lust as he thought about what he'd find if he lifted that skirt. Not that he'd do it here. Oh no, he'd wait until they were alone, to when he could have her all to himself.

Volatile energy arced between them, and Brad was certain anyone within a fifty-mile radius could feel it. But then suddenly her brow furrowed, and when her body stiffened, he jerked his hand back. From her reactions it was clear she didn't want anyone to know what they were doing behind closed doors. Which, come to think of it, had been his intention all along as well.

"Hey, Sophie," Brad greeted when she turned curious eyes on him. Not wanting to give her friend the wrong idea about his relationship—or lack thereof—with Madison, he said in a casual tone, "I just wanted to let you know that Bandit and I are heading to Granddad's nursing home for a quick visit, and I didn't want you to think I'd forgotten about your plumbing."

"What's wrong with your plumbing?" Sophie asked.

"The shower," Madison started and paused, a blush creeping up her neck like she was remembering how she'd taken him in her mouth. Christ knows he hadn't stopped thinking about it.

The ever-astute Sophie eyed Madison, then glanced at Brad, a knowing look on her face. "What happened? Did the pipes blow or something?"

Madison sucked in a quick breath and Brad stifled a groan. Leave it to Sophie to nail the hammer on the head.

He cleared his throat. "Yeah, something like that." He rocked back and forth on his feet, like a guilty kid caught with his hand in the cookie jar.

"Why don't I come with you," Madison piped in, bending forward to pat Bandit, who leaned into her. "I'd love to see Granddad, and the bakery is closed for the day anyway. Which means I'm free until the fireworks later tonight."

Sophie held her hands up, palms out, a strange almost worried look in her eyes. "Yeah, well, with the way you two are sparking, I'm pretty sure something is going to explode long before that."

After spending a glorious afternoon at the nursing home and loving how happy Granddad was to see Brad, they returned home to work on the plumbing. Madison assisted Brad, learning more about copper fittings and shutoff valves than she'd ever wanted to know. Once they were done, they shared a pizza at her small kitchen table, talking quietly about their afternoon visit and how well Granddad seemed to be doing after his last incident.

Even though she wanted to ask him about Jocelyn and the intense conversation he seemed to be having with her earlier that day, she closed her mouth. They weren't in a relationship, which meant it wasn't her business, even though it made her feel insanely jealous. And of course she couldn't forget the way Jocelyn was watching Brad's every movement, especially when he made his way toward her. The seething look Jocelyn had given her after Brad had lifted her from the stands had Madison's body stiffening and the smile falling from her face. It was that look and the determination behind it that told Madison one thing and one thing only: Jocelyn wanted him back. As she thought about that her stomach plummeted, even though she knew better than to hope for more with Brad. Madison knew she could never compete with a svelte, put-together girl like his ex. One who was comfortable in her own skin and knew how to walk, talk and use her body to get what she wanted.

"Everything okay?" Brad asked as he eyed her from across the small table, their knees touching intimately in the dim light.

She swallowed the last of her pizza and plastered on a smile. "Of course. I have running water again."

"Yeah, but who knows for how long. You really do need to think about finding a new place, you know."

"You're one to talk," she returned as she grabbed his empty plate and placed it on hers.

"At least I have air conditioning," he teased.

"Seriously though, Brad, you live like a nomad."

He shrugged. "Like I said, I'm not around enough to bother."

"Yeah, but surely when you come back from being away, you'd like to come back to a nice place, with things that make you feel at home and make you feel happy."

He stood to help her with the dishes, and the way he turned the conversation back to her didn't go unnoticed. "Are you and Jonah going to look for a new place when he comes back?"

"I'd like to."

"Where are you thinking of looking?"

She pursed her lips and thought more about it. "I'm not sure." She walked to the counter and placed the dishes in the sink, deciding to wash them later. "Since I hate moving, and it's an incredible amount of work to turn the main level of a house into a storefront, I guess I'd just like to move into my forever home. Somewhere in a nice neighborhood, where there are good schools and a lot of downtown foot traffic for my business."

"Your forever home?"

"Yeah, a place where I could raise a family upstairs and keep my business on the ground floor." She shrugged. "But a place like that is hard to find, and even if I did find one, I'd never be able to afford it anyway."

"So you want a family?"

"Eventually.

Brad went unusually quiet as he listened, and as he looked pointedly at her, she got the sense his thoughts were a million miles away. Getting the uneasy feeling that Sophie was right, and something really was going on with him, she opened her mouth to ask, but he cut her off and he gave her a playful whack on the ass.

"You'd better get changed. The temperature is dropping tonight and I don't want you to get cold at the fairgrounds after the sun goes down."

She nodded, and turned toward her bedroom, but before she could go, Brad grabbed her arm and spun her back around. He pulled her close and as sparks arced between, she wondered if they'd even make it to the fireworks, or if they were going to stay in and create their own. But as an American military man, she knew Brad would want to go out of respect for fallen comrades and for those soldiers still serving.

He dipped his head and planted a warm kiss on her mouth, one that felt more emotional than physical, and completely caught her off guard. After he inched away, she drew in a breath and asked, "What was that for?"

"For helping me at the nursing home, and for helping out

the band kids."

"Then I should be the one kissing you."

"Oh," he said.

"If it wasn't for you, I never would have been able to bake all those cupcakes."

"You're right." He had a wicked grin on his face. "You should be the one kissing me. In fact," he added, "I think I'll hold you to that later tonight. But right now we need to get a move on it if we want to get a good seat."

She laughed and was about to head to her room, when he put his mouth close to her ear and whispered, "Oh, and don't forget. No panties."

A shiver moved through her when she heard the lust in his voice. After hurrying to her room, she changed into a pair of jeans and blouse and grabbed a sweater from her closet. She gave herself a once over in the mirror, and oddly enough, knowing she had no panties on, knowing that was how Brad wanted her, made her feel sexy, naughty. She looked at her curvy hips and abundant cleavage, suddenly feeling less conscious about herself. Even though she was pretending to be something she wasn't, she couldn't deny that under Brad's care she could feel herself becoming less and less self-conscious.

She grabbed a blanket on the way out the door and hopped into Brad's truck. They drove through the city and less than fifteen minutes later he pulled into a parking spot at the fairgrounds. They strolled through the crowd, Brad staying close to her side as they maneuvered through the throngs. A local band played music and the scent of popcorn filled the air as kids chased one another. They bumped into Josh, who, after he pointed out where everyone was sitting, turned to Madison.

"Hey, Madison," he said. "My cousin told me you made all the cupcakes for her band's fundraising." When Madison nodded, he stepped a bit closer, and dipped his head. "That was a nice thing you did." He rubbed his stomach. "And they were delicious."

"I'm glad you liked them."

"Maybe I'll stop by the bakery this week to see what other things you have on the menu."

"I'd love for you to come by. I'll make you something special."

He smiled. "I'd like that."

She felt Brad step closer to her, his hand brushing hers in a possessive manner. She turned in time to catch the dangerous way he was glaring at Josh.

Josh, as though oblivious to the deadly stare, ignored Brad and said, "I'll see you later then, Madison."

After he left, Brad put his hand on the small of her back and guided her through the crowd. She looked up at him, taking in his hard profile, and the dark, contemplative look on his face. What the hell? Maybe Sophie was right, and something really was going on with him.

"Brad?" she began.

"Yeah?" His features softened when he aimed his glance her way, and her heart lurched in her chest.

"What's wrong?" she asked, wrapping her arms around herself when a cool breeze came out of nowhere and washed over her.

"Nothing," he said and stopped walking. His hands went to her shoulders, and when he tightened her sweater around her body, her knees nearly gave out. Oh, God, she was in way over her head with him. "How about we grab a spot over there." He pointed to a secluded area in the fair grounds.

"You don't want to sit with your friends?"

He ran his hands down her arms, and her pulse leapt. In a voice that was low, he said, "I think I want you all to myself tonight."

They walked to the secluded area and she laid out her blanket. Brad dropped down beside her and she became acutely aware of his closeness, acutely aware of the way her body was humming, eager to get naked with him again. As she hugged herself and scanned the crowd, she thought back to earlier that morning, to the way he forced her to expose herself to him. She couldn't believe the way he made her feel so sexy as he indulged in her naked body.

A warm quiver moved through her as she caught Brad's gaze. His eyes locked on hers and they shared a secret smile, one that set her body on fire and had her breathing a little quicker.

As they sat there in comfortable silence, just enjoying each other's company, a few more people came and threw their blankets down next to them. A short while later, the fireworks started, and with darkness obscuring their identities, Madison leaned in to him. He put his arm around her and as he held her, rubbing his hand up and down her arm to create heat, a barrage of emotions moved through her. Her heart leapt and she swallowed against the tightness in her throat. Honestly, she'd never felt so close to him before, and quite frankly, was annoyed with herself for letting her emotions get the better of her.

Refusing to dwell on the things he made her feel, she concentrated only on the pretty display lighting up the night sky. When the fireworks were over, Brad climbed to his feet, and hauled her up with him. Her body collided with his, and as everyone gathered up their blankets, he put his mouth close to her ear. "I think I'm ready for that kiss."

"Here?" she asked.

He glanced around and she could feel the tension in his body. "Probably not a good idea, but Jesus, Madison, I want you so much, I'm not sure I can make it back to your place."

Butterflies filled her stomach. "You do?"

"Fuck yeah, I do," he growled, looking a little rugged, a little dangerous.

She grabbed the blanket, and bundled it in her arms, her entire body quivering in anticipation. "Then let's hurry."

They rushed back to Brad's truck, and as they drove through town, his hand crept across the cab to capture hers. Every few minutes he kept glancing her way, and she wished he wouldn't, because the hungry, predatory look in his eyes made it hard for her to breathe.

What felt like an eternity later, they pulled into her parking lot, and Brad climbed from the truck. She slid from her seat and met him at the front of the vehicle.

She fished her key from her purse, and Brad took it from her. They entered through the café door, and his hand closed over hers once they were inside. Silence ensued as he led her up the stairs to her apartment on the top level. They walked to her bedroom and after they entered, Brad shut the door behind them, leaving the lights on.

He turned to her. His eyes skirted over her body and she made a strangled noise, the sound bringing his attention back to her face.

"You're so beautiful."

When she didn't say anything, he eyed her with suspicion. "What's wrong?" he asked.

She looked down, and even though being with him made her feel more confident in her physical appearance, deep inside she was still just a laid-back homebody at heart, one who was more comfortable in her glasses and easy-fitting clothes. And of course she couldn't forget the fact that she slept with a bite plate.

If only he thought that girl was beautiful...

"You don't believe me?"

"Brad—"

"I don't think you realize how beautiful you are," he

murmured, his voice caressing her all over, the desire in his eyes touching the depths of her soul. "Jesus, Madison. I thought I was going to have to kill Josh tonight."

"What are you talking about?"

"Didn't you see the way he was looking at you?"

She shook her head. "No, not really."

Brad scrubbed his hand over his jaw. "Come here."

She moved toward him and he met her halfway. He spun her around to face the rectangular mirror over her bureau and pressed his chest to her back.

"Look at yourself."

"I'm looking," she responded, barely able to concentrate as his erection caressed her back, letting her know in no uncertain terms that he did indeed find her physically beautiful.

"Do you not see what I see? Feel what I feel?" He pulled her hair from her shoulders, then ran his hand along her lush curves.

Her body quivered beneath his touch and when he feathered his hot mouth along her neck she began trembling. His hands trailed along her sides, then he inched back to pull her sweater from her shoulders, a low growl of longing rising up from his throat.

As sexual energy leapt between them, he brushed the underside of her breasts through her blouse, then met her eyes in the mirror. "Your turn," he murmured.

"My turn?"

"Yeah." He grabbed her hands and placed them on her body. "Time for you to see and feel for yourself."

She gasped, every nerve in her body coming alive as shocked silence lingered. Moisture broke out on her body, and she held his gaze in the mirror as she tried to wrap her brain around this unexpected turn of events. Good God, exposing herself to him this morning was one thing, but touching herself in front of him, in front of a mirror was something else entirely. Then again, she *had* done it once, when she'd thought she was dreaming. Which meant that maybe, just maybe between the sheets she wasn't really pretending to be something she wasn't. Maybe she really was brazen at heart, and it took the right guy to help her free that side of herself.

"Do it," he said, his voice coaxing, the look in his eyes urging her to shed the last of her inhibition and do what he was asking. She stood there trying to catch her breath as the air around them grew heavy.

"Madison," he said, his voice a little harsher, a little more demanding, fueling the flames in her belly. "Take your clothes off."

Good God, there really was something about his take-charge attitude that got to her. When he crushed his body to hers, she trembled from head to toe, wanting...no...needing to do this. Not just for him, but for herself. Her fingers went to her blouse. Slowly, one by one, she released the buttons, and when she felt him suck in a breath, his chest expanding as it pressed against her back, it filled her with a new kind of bravado.

She released the last button and rolled one shoulder. The blouse slipped down her arm and Brad grabbed it, his fingers trailing over her flesh as he pulled it off and let it drop to the floor. She slipped off her bra straps and her nipples tightened painfully as Brad swiped his tongue over his bottom lip. With no darkness to hide her body, she pulled off her bra to expose her big breasts, ones she spent so many years hiding. She put her hands on them, and Brad moaned, desire growing in his eyes.

She cradled her breasts, and as she enjoyed the weight in her hands, all the while listening to Brad's agonized moans behind her, she couldn't deny that she felt desirable, feminine even, under his watchful eye. She angled her body, and examined her breasts from the side, lightly rubbing her thumbs over her nipples as she took pleasure in the texture and size.

Sliding her hands lower, and catching the urgency on Brad's face, the raw desire in his eyes as she undressed, she pulled open her jeans and wiggled slightly as she slid them down. A quiver moved through her when Brad ran his hands over the crest of her buttocks, the gentle pressure urging her on.

"Mmmm, no panties," he said, his voice fractured, broken, heavy with desire. "Do you have any idea how crazy it made me tonight, sitting next to you for hours and knowing you were bare for me?"

After removing her jeans, she straightened and looked at her nakedness in the mirror, her body flooding with sexual heat.

"Touch yourself," Brad growled, impatience in his tone.

She put her hands on her stomach and moved them to her sides, shaping her contours.

Brad watched her carefully, then said, "Open your legs."

She inched her legs open, the warm air rushing over the moisture between her thighs as she registered every curve in her body. Calloused fingers trailed down her arm, and when her eyes met his in the mirror, raw lust filled his gaze. As she looked at him, every square inch of her skin burned, her breasts felt heavy, achy...and oddly enough...beautiful.

"You have a body to be admired, sweetheart. Not hidden." His hands reached her hips and he gripped them hard, his fingers biting into her skin. "At least not from me."

Her body spasmed with pleasure as his words rang in her ears. Without his coaxing, she touched the inside of her thighs, and couldn't believe how much pleasure she was taking in the exploring her body, how freeing and erotic it felt to caress herself like this.

"That's it," he said, his voice a hoarse whisper as his cock pulsed against her back. As sexual tension hung heavy, he murmured, "Touch every inch of yourself."

She moaned, and when she ran her finger over her slit, her head fell back, landing on his chest. Ecstasy like she'd never before experienced swamped her as she concentrated only on the points of pleasure. Her warm heat coated her finger and she grew slicker as she rubbed herself, circling her clit until it was hard and needy and desperate for Brad's attention.

With Brad's mouth close to her ear, he whispered, "Look at your pussy, baby. Look at how wet and hot it is." She lifted her head and let her glance drop to the juncture between her legs. "You like it, don't you? You like touching yourself?"

Her finger moved quicker over her sex and when she didn't say anything, Brad pushed, "Tell me, Madison. Tell me how much you like touching your pussy."

"Oh, God, Brad. I like it," she murmured. "I like it so much."

He curled his hands around her waist. "Yeah, I like it too." He pushed his cock into the small of her back, and lowered his voice, his breath hot on her neck when he said, "Feel how much I like it, baby?"

Pleasure forked through her and she smiled, loving that she could do this to him. She slipped a finger inside herself and she felt his body tense, his cock pulsing hard against her back. Her throat dried as she stroked herself, acquainting herself with her body, one she'd always shied away from touching. But not tonight. Oh no, tonight with Brad urging her on, not only was she caressing herself for the first time in her life, she was taking pleasure in the way her body looked and felt.

Tension grew inside her, and her finger worked harder over her clit. She grabbed Brad's hand. "Touch with me."

One of Brad hands went to her breasts to play with her

nipples while the other hand joined hers between her legs. His palm closed over the back of her hand and heat radiated from his body to hers as one of his thick fingers pushed inside to join with hers. Feeling so deliciously full, she began moving, rocking against their fingers while he toyed with her nipples, the dual assault pushing her over the edge.

"Oh God, Brad," she cried out when her skin tightened, heat streaking through her with the rapid approach of her climax.

"You are so sexy when you come," Brad whispered.

She flushed hotly, then shook all over, giving herself over to the powerful orgasm ripping through her. She whimpered and kept her hand between her legs as she rode out the waves. Warmth reverberated through her as Brad held her tight, absorbing her tremors. When she stopped spasming, she sucked in air, but before she could catch her breath, Brad spun her around, and lifted her clear off the floor.

"I need to be inside you," he growled as he set her on her dresser. Her heart beat madly as she listened to the impatience in his voice. She looked at him, and not only was he shaking, it occurred to her that she'd never seen such intensity in his eyes before.

His glance left hers and fell over her body. Strong fingers gripped her thighs and roughly pushed them open, completely exposing her to him. He pulled open her nether lips. "So fucking pretty." He lightly brushed her sensitive clit, and when her hips jerked, the muscles along his jaw rippled. Soft curses caught in his throat as he ripped open his jeans and shoved them to his thigh. "Jesus Christ, I need to fuck you so bad."

Her dry throat cracked as she tore at his shirt. "I need it too," she managed to get out. He pulled off his shirt and a second later, after he pulled a condom from his pocket and rolled it on, he positioned his cock at her entrance.

She jerked her hips forward, demanding more as she palmed his shoulder muscles and found him trembling. His mouth devoured hers hungrily, and he kissed her hard, his tongue pushing inside to tangle with hers. Pressure built in her body as she met his every thrust, and as they established a rhythm, the world around her faded. Nothing existing but this moment and this man.

She writhed, shockwaves moving through her body as his fingers went to her inflamed clit. He stroked her gently, then a gasp caught in her throat when he powered his cock into her, driving so hard and deep she could barely remember her name.

She held him tight and her body suffused with color as he pushed deeper, harder, like he was seeking more than release. She scraped her nails over his back and filled her lungs with his scent, letting it curl through her and raise her passion to new heights. He dipped his head and swiped his tongue across one sensitized nipple and when he glanced back at her his expression was tender, hot.

Her breath caught and she cried out his name. His mouth found hers again and a riot of emotions broke out inside her.

As she savored the warmth of his mouth, a whimper escaped her lips. He pulled his cock almost all the way out, and when he rammed back in her body went up in flames, an orgasm taking her by surprise. He swallowed her gasp as she squeezed her sex muscles as her hot flow of release dripped over his cock. The pleasure was so intense she gripped his shoulders, sure she was going to black out.

"Christ," he groaned, closing his eyes in distress as her pussy muscles gripped him hard. He began panting, his breath coming in labored bursts and she could hear the impatience, the need in his voice when he said, "I'm not going to last, baby."

She put her palms on his face, and his eyes opened. God,

when he looked directly at her like that, it was possible to forget every sane thought.

"I want to feel you come inside me," she whispered. "I want you to feel as good as I do."

The sound of him swallowing cut through the air, then he gripped her thighs, pulled her closer to the edge of her bureau, and burrowed so deep, her womb clenched. As the air around them grew heavy with the scent of their lovemaking, he wrapped his arms around her waist, thrust once, twice, then threw his head back and let go on a growl.

She moaned as he pulsed inside her, and she squeezed him hard, milking his release as her heart beat erratically in her chest.

"Fuck," he murmured into her neck, his warm breath arousing her all over again. After a long time, he eased his cock out, and disposed of the condom.

He kicked off his pants, stepped back between her legs, and slid an arm around her waist. "Come on." He pulled her off the dresser, his expression so dark, so concentrated and so potent it touched something deep inside her.

With her body still humming, she fought to think. "Where are we going?"

His nostrils flared and as he intimately ran his fingers down her arm she shivered under his touch. His gaze dropped from her eyes, to her mouth to her breasts, and she heard the raw hunger in his voice when he said, "I'm not nearly done with you, sweetheart."

She fell silent as he scooped her up and carried her to her bed. An uneasy feeling closed in on her as he spread her out and climbed over her body, because she knew she was far from done with him too. But Brad had made it perfectly clear that he was offering only a month of sex. And while he wasn't looking for anything that resembled a relationship, she found herself hungering for so much more than just his touch.

10

Warm morning sunlight filtered in through Madison's open curtains as Brad stretched out on the bed. He shifted to his side and his cock swelled the second he set sight on the gorgeous woman asleep next to him. He went up on one elbow for a better look. As he gazed at her, taking in her nakedness, her mussed hair, and the traces of makeup still on her face because he refused to let her out of the bed last night, he knew he had to have her again.

She stirred beside him, and when her eyes opened and she caught him staring down at her, she made a move to jump from the mattress, something he'd grown accustomed to.

"I'll be right back," she said an anxious look on her face as she smoothed her hands through her hair.

"Where do you think you're going?" Brad asked, dragging her back down with him. He rolled on top of her, pinning her beneath him.

She pointed to the hall. "I was just going to fresh..." Her voice fell off as he pushed his knee between her legs, opening her to him.

"And I was just going to fuck you," he murmured. She gasped as he positioned his cock at her entrance. He gave her a sheepish look. "That is if you're not too sore from last night."

"I'm not," she murmured. Her eyes dimmed with desire, and something else, something he couldn't quite put a name to when she wrapped her hands around his neck and opened her body to him.

He pushed into her, driving his cock all the way inside her. As her tight muscles closed around him, he buried his face in her neck. Jesus, everything about their lovemaking felt so intimate, so right, but he somehow knew no matter how many times they came together as one, he'd never be able to assuage his need for her.

"Brad," she murmured, everything in the soft, intimate way she spoke his name, touching him on a completely different level. A moan caught in her throat, and her body quivered.

She wrapped her legs around his back and held him tight as he pumped deep. Their moans of pleasure merged, her hard nipples scraping against his chest as he settled his weight on her. She whimpered and arched her back, running her nails along his shoulders as he ravaged her.

"I love the way you fill me, Brad," she cried out.

"I know, baby. I know." As a barrage of emotions ripped through him, some small coherent part of his brain registered that sex with her was always good, but there was something different about this time. Something that was making it harder and harder for him to separate sex and emotions.

Silence fell over them as they both gave and took, communicating through their touches only. They both pushed and pulled, increasing the rhythm and pressure, knowing just what the other one needed to bring them to orgasm. Even after all the sex they had last night, both their climaxes came fast, and as moisture sealed their bodies, he collapsed on top of her.

"Jesus, Madison," he murmured into her neck, his chest rising and falling erratically. He inched back and smoothed her hair from her forehead, and when he caught her glance, his eyes moved over face. A moment later his stomach dropped, and he rolled off her. "Shit."

"What?" she asked, her body tensing as her hand once again went to her hair to smooth it down.

He angled his head to see her. "We didn't use a condom."

Her eyes lit with surprise, then her hand closed over his. The warmth and familiarity in her touch escalated the tension inside him. "It's okay. I'm on the pill, remember."

"Yeah, I remember."

She crinkled her nose. "Actually, I was kind of wondering why you went back to using one. I mean, we're protected and we accidently went without one the first night..."

As she let her words fall off, he pulled her to him. She snuggled into him and his nerve endings came alive. Deep down, he knew he was getting in too deep with her. And somehow, he just somehow knew, making love to her for the rest of the month, without a barrier in place, one that helped him keep a measure of distance, not only physically, but emotionally, was going to change everything for him.

He threw his legs over the bed. "I...uh...I need to get moving." He raked his hands through his hair and shot her a look over his shoulder. "The realtor is coming by to assess Granddad's place."

A surprised look came over her face. "It's going on the market already?"

"Yeah. I'd like to at least get it up for sale before I leave at the end of the month."

"Right," Madison said as she stared at the mussed sheets. She wet her lips and her thoughts seemed to be a million miles away when she added, "I suppose it's good to tie up all loose ends before you go."

His gaze moved over her face as she reached for her lip balm on her nightstand, and he felt an odd tightness in his gut. Is that what she thought of him? A loose end to be tied up at the end of the month? Really, why wouldn't she? With that last thought in mind, he slipped from the bed, pulled on his clothes and left in a hurry.

For the next few weeks Brad worked on getting the house ready for sale, and when he wasn't at the old homestead he could be found at Madison's place, finishing her repairs, helping her replace the old copper piping and seal the holes in the walls.

They cooked together every night, talked quietly over their dinner, and last weekend she even helped him pick out a gift for the baby shower. For that he was grateful, considering there was a good chance he'd have showed up with a screw-driver set or something equally pathetic. Every night, however, he fell into bed with Madison, where they'd make sweet love until the wee hours of the morning, taking advantage of every moment they had, while they still had it.

As he looked at her now, on this beautiful Sunday morning, he realized that going to bed with her every night was one thing, but waking up with her every morning was something else entirely, something he was getting awfully used to it. Except the month was quickly coming to a close, and in a few short days he'd be heading north and his brother would be moving back in to take over where Brad had left off. Well...not exactly where Brad had left off. At least he hoped not. Not that he had any rights with Madison. He didn't. And the truth was, she could date whomever she wanted.

As Madison stretched out beside him, he glanced at the clock. They'd been up half the night making love and if he didn't tear his eyes off her naked body and get his shit together, he'd be late for the baby shower.

"Hey," he said, and when she turned to him, looking all sleepy, sexy...a well-fucked woman...his cock hardened. He smiled and as she rubbed up against him he had to admit, he loved how comfortable she now was in her own skin, how she no longer hid under the cover of darkness, or ran away every morning only to come back completely made up. His smile dissolved when he thought about walking away when this thing between them was over.

"What's wrong?" Madison asked, blinking dark lashes at him.

He pointed to the clock. "I have to get ready for Gemma's baby shower."

"And that's a problem?"

He ran his hand down her arm, and gently stroked the underside of her breast, loving the way her nipples tightened beneath his touch. "It's a problem because all I want to do is fuck you again."

A smile split her lips and the emotional way she looked at him nearly stopped his heart. Christ, there was no denying that he felt a new closeness between them, an intimacy that went well beyond sex.

As she adjusted her body, offering herself up to him so nicely, he climbed over her and dropped a soft kiss on her mouth. "Baby, if I don't move now, I'm never going to." His cock probed her opening, anxious to nestle deep inside.

"Then I guess you should move," she murmured, a wicked glint in her eyes as she wiggled her hips, her passion drenched pussy closing around the tip of his cock, urging him to move inside her.

"Fuck," he murmured, his mouth going to her breast. He kissed her nipple, and her skin tightened beneath his lips.

She grinned. "Exactly."

Her hand slid over his back, and he moaned, allowing himself to get lost in her touch. "A fast one?" he asked.

"And hard," she said.

"Jesus girl, you're going to be the death of me." Without preamble, he thrust inside her. As his bare cock made contact with her hot flesh, he knew it was going to be a fast time indeed, and no matter how many times he fucked her, he'd never be able to get enough.

Her eyes fell shut as he moved in and out of her, and the ecstasy flitting across her face was just about the most beautiful thing he'd ever seen. His heart pinched, some working brain cell warning that being with her like this felt too real, too good.

Shit. The last thing he wanted to do was fall for her. He hit the road in few short days, and past experiences told him not to set himself up for failure again. And of course, he couldn't forget how she was doing a countdown of her own, showing no signs of wanting more once their thirty days were over.

"Brad," she murmured, her mouth opening and closing as she tumbled into orgasm. Her pussy squeezed him and his mouth found hers as he too gave himself over, joining her in climax.

After their tremors subsided, he slid off and she glanced at the clock. Trying to keep things light he said, "What, now you're timing me?"

She laughed. "No, just making sure you can still make it on time."

He frowned, and she closed her palm over his cheek, the warmth of her hand, not to mention the compassion on her face, touching him in places so deep, a tremor moved through him.

"You don't want to go, do you?" she asked.

He cleared his throat and tried for normal. "It's for

couples, mainly, but Gemma wants me there, and I'd never do anything to disappoint her."

Warmth moved into her eyes, and the way she smiled up at him left him feeling breathless. "Would it help if I went with you?"

His eyes moved over her face, and his heart squeezed to think she'd do that for him, even knowing Jack's girlfriend could very well be there. "You don't have to do that."

"Maybe I want to."

He brought her hand to her face and kissed her fingers. "It could be...awkward."

She nodded, knowing full what he meant. "A lot has changed, Brad."

As he looked at her, he knew she was right. Right before his eyes he watched her change, blossom into a confident woman, and he couldn't help but think he was partially responsible. In fact, he hoped he was.

"If you want me to go, I'll go."

He swallowed against the tightness in his throat, knowing he wanted her there, and not because he found the whole idea of attending a baby shower solo uncomfortable. "I'd love it if you came."

"Good." She gave him a playful wink. "Otherwise I'd be stuck at home eating a whole cake by myself."

He thought back to yesterday, to when he'd dragged her upstairs with him. She'd been putting the final touches on a cake. Little did he know she'd been baking it for Gemma and Cole, people she barely knew.

He shook his head, because she never failed to surprise him, impress him with her generosity and thoughtfulness. "So you were planning to come all along?"

She smiled. "Gemma did invite me. But I wasn't going to go if you didn't want me there." She gave him a nudge. "Now come on, we don't want to be late."

They hopped from the bed, showered together, grabbed a bite for breakfast and made their way to Gemma and Cole's cute little bungalow on the outskirts of town. In the yard they were greeted by their dogs, Stallone, Charlie and Nana. After Madison and Brad dropped to their knees, showering all three animals with attention—although the dogs seemed more interested in what Madison had in the cake box than in their pats—they walked up the pathway leading to the front door.

"Brad," Gemma said as she swung the door open. But her attention quickly turned to Madison and the box in her hand. "Madison, I'm so glad you came. But you didn't have to bring anything."

"I wanted to," she said, and as Brad stepped closer in a protective manner, one hand going to the small of her back he suddenly knew...knew what it was about her that had been getting under his skin, and had him thinking about long term. She was sexy, sensitive, fun loving and compassionate. Everything he'd ever wanted in a partner.

"Come on in and meet everyone." She ushered them both inside and took the gift from Brad before she pointed to the kitchen. "The guys are in there. Go grab a beer while I introduce Madison around."

Brad glanced at Madison, gauging her reactions. She smoothed her hand over her pretty sundress, one with a plunging necklace that showcased her beautiful curvy body. Even though his protective instincts were coming out full force, she nodded, and sent him on his way. Brad joined Jack and Cole in the kitchen, but his attention was on Madison as Gemma introduced her around.

Madison exchanged greetings with a few couples he recognized and a few he didn't. When she came to Jack's girlfriend, Sarah, he watched the way Sarah's envious eyes moved over Madison's lush body. That's when it occurred to him the girl was completely jealous of Madison, which was probably why she'd picked on her. For a minute he wondered why Jack would date a girl like her. Then he remembered Jack's father was a general, and from the looks of her expensive jewelry, the two likely moved in the same social circles.

"Hello, Maddy," Sarah said, her glance moving over Madison's pretty dress.

Tension moved through Brad, but when Madison straightened her shoulders, standing her ground and facing her childhood bully straight on, he relaxed, and released the breath he had no idea he was holding.

"It's Madison," she said politely. "I probably should have told you that a long time ago."

Brad smiled, never more proud of anyone in his entire life. Not only was she sweet and sexy, she was classy and dignified, handling the situation like the poised beautiful woman she was.

"Hey," Cole said, putting his hand on Brad's shoulder to bring his attention back around. "What's the matter with you?" he asked, looking past Brad's shoulders to see what he'd been staring at.

"Nothing." He took a huge swig of beer.

"Don't worry," Cole said. "She's in good hands."

"Yeah, that's not what I heard," Jack said, a knowing grin on his face.

"Who's in good hands?" Garrett came into the room, his fiancée, Tallulah, beside him. Brad smiled at his best friend, then turned his attention to Tallulah, thinking how good the two looked together as he took note of her small baby bump.

"How are you feeling?" he asked.

When Tallulah smiled and leaned in to Garrett, there was so much love on her face it damn near took Brad's his breath away. That look had something niggling in the pit of his gut, something he couldn't quite put his finger on.

"Never happier," Tallulah said, rubbing her hands over her stomach. Garrett dipped his head to give her a kiss, and Brad's stomach took that moment to nosedive. He was happy for Garrett, he really was, but he couldn't help but feel a pang of envy that his friend had found love and happiness, the one thing Brad had always wanted and was certain he could never have. His brain took that moment to think back to his ex's betrayal and as the memories shook him, he finished off his beer.

Garrett eyed him, then glanced in to the other room. "Why don't you grab me a seat, babe. I'll be right in, okay?"

After Tallulah slipped from the kitchen, Garrett turned to Brad and folded his arms. "Want to talk about it?"

"There's nothing to talk about." He reached for another bottle.

"Oh really?" Garrett questioned, his expression skeptical. "Then what the hell have you been doing for the last month? Hibernating? Winter's not here yet, pal."

Knowing he could never keep anything from Garrett, but not wanting to talk about the deeper emotions he was feeling for Madison, not only because he was too goddamn confused about them himself, but this was neither the time nor place.

But he knew Garrett wouldn't back down without an explanation so he said, "I've been working on Granddad's house. I wanted to get it listed before I leave."

"I stopped by your place a few times and you weren't there. You don't even answer your cell anymore."

He took a pull from his bottle. "I've been staying at Madison's, helping her around her place while Jonah is away. Besides," he added, gesturing with a nod toward Tallulah in the other room, "you had your own issues to work out."

"So there's nothing going on between you two?" Josh asked, coming into the kitchen from the back door.

Before he could answer, Gemma called them all into the

living room to play games and open gifts. He soon found himself eating cake and playing board games that required them to divulge intimate information—sexual information—but after a while he relaxed into the afternoon, enjoying the laughter and camaraderie. After the presents were unwrapped, and the food was devoured, Madison excused herself and made her way into the kitchen to refresh her drink.

When Brad saw Josh follow behind her, he climbed from his seat, a wave of possession zinging through his blood. As he made his way toward them, he could hear their voices spilling into the hallway.

"I thought I'd come by the bakery again," Josh said. "I'm still dreaming about your sticky buns."

What the fuck...

"They're new on the menu, so I'm glad you liked them."

Brad drove his hands into his pocket and leaned against the doorjamb to watch the exchange. Silence fell heavy for a second as Madison poured soda into her cup. When she turned back to Josh, he angled his head and asked, "So, you and Brad...you're just friends?"

At the mention of his name Brad stepped farther in the room to make his presence known, and Madison swung her head his way, her long hair flying around her shoulders as her eyes locked with his. The scent of her shampoo wafted before his nose. He breathed it in, and as he thought about how he'd washed his hair with it earlier that morning, along with all the other naughtier things they'd done in the shower, she went quiet, like she was waiting for him to say something.

But what the hell was he supposed to say? That they were just friends, friends with benefits? And that he'd offered her thirty days in bed, and she'd readily agreed. Emotions churned inside him as he mulled that over. Christ, what kind of an asshole set those kinds of terms in a relationship, especially with a sweet girl like her. When he continued to stand there, his mouth clamped shut, Madison turned her focus back to Josh.

She aimed a smile Josh's way, but her voice sounded tight when she said, "He's staying at my place to help with repairs while Jonah is away. We've had a lot of plumbing disasters lately, and Brad, well...he's good with his hands."

Brad nearly swallowed his tongue as he thought about all the things he'd been doing with his hands, not to mention his tongue and his cock. Jesus, just thinking about it now had him hardening.

"And you and Jonah?" Josh asked, interested clear in his eyes as he inched closer. "I thought—"

"Friends," she said. "And roommate. When he gets back in a couple of days, he'll be moving back in and Brad will be leaving." She swung her head back toward him again, thick lashes blinking rapidly over her dark eyes. "Isn't that right, Brad?"

"What?" he asked, his thoughts racing a million miles an hour.

"You'll be leaving in a few short days," she said.

Brad drove his hand into his pocket, his blood flowing thick and heavy through his veins as she held his gaze. "Yeah, that's right," he said, not bothering to mask the hardness in his tone as she reminded him of their timeline.

Josh stepped closer to her, a wolfish smile on his face as he deliberately moved into her personal space. In that instant, Brad realized just how much he wanted to keep Madison all to himself, how dangerously close he was to falling for her. Not to mention how much he wanted to beat the living shit out of Josh just for talking to her. After all, she could talk to and date whomever she wanted to, right?

Jesus Christ, he was in so much fucking trouble.

"What's gotten in to you?" Sophie asked. But before Madison could answer, Sophie gave her a teasing wink. "Never mind. I already know."

Madison untied her apron and forced a smile, even though she had a killer headache, compliments of her TMJ. "Do you ever stop?"

As though picking up on her unease, the smile fell from Sophie's face. "Speaking of stopping, Brad leaves tonight, right?"

Madison glanced at the clock. "Yeah." She walked to the door, switched the sign to *Closed*, then poured herself a much-needed mug of her favorite herbal tea, one that would hopefully calm her nerves. She grabbed two pain pills from her purse, chased them with her tea, then lowered herself into one of the bakery chairs, all the while trying not to let her emotions get the better of her. Trying to keep the conversation light she went on to explain, "He had some last minute things to take care of with the house, and will be stopping by shortly to grab his gear."

Sophie dropped down into the chair next to her, her brow knit together in a frown. "And you're going to just end it?" She snapped her fingers. "Just like that?"

Madison blew on her tea, took another sip and went on to say, "I told you, we agreed to one month of sex and that's it."

"Yeah, but Madison, I know you want more. It's written all over your face."

"I know, but..." She stopped talking and massaged her aching jaw. Even though she was broken hearted that Brad was going to walk away tonight, at least she could start wearing her bite plate again. Lord knows her dentist was going to kill her for going without her device for so long. She swallowed uneasily, not even wanting to think what kind of damage she'd done to her dry, sensitive eyes with the extended use of her contracts. The specialist hadn't even wanted her to use them in the first place.

"But what?" Sophie went quiet for a moment, then said, "You don't think he's going to like the Madison that Jonah and I know, right?" She reached out, pulled Madison's hand away from her jaw, and gave a reassuring squeeze. "The one hidden behind all the dressy clothes and makeup you've been wearing?" Madison's head jerked up with a start, and when she met shrewd eyes that knew her every dark secret she exhaled slowly. "Don't think I haven't noticed," Sophie went on to say. "For the past month you've been scratching at your eyes and eating soft foods because your jaw is killing you."

"I just...I didn't want him to see that side of me."

"Why?"

She waved her hand over her body and smoothed her palm over her hair. "Because this is the girl Brad slept with."

Sophie squeezed her hand. "You seem to like that girl now too. Over the last month I've watched you change and you clearly have a lot more confidence in yourself and in your body. I'm guessing Brad had something to do with that."

She went quiet thinking about the way he made her strip bare in the mirror, the way he urged her to touch and admire herself. Okay, so clearly he liked her body, helped *her* like her body, to become more comfortable in her own skin, but she wanted him to like the girl beneath the body. The girl who wanted to kick back on Sundays, read the paper with her glasses on, put her bite plate in at night and didn't always want to be Made-Up-Madison.

"Why don't you take that new confidence and go after what you want? Show Brad the other side of Madison. I think you might like the end results."

"And if I scare him off?"

"Believe me, you won't."

Madison took a moment to chew on that, thinking how early on in the relationship she used to get up early in the morning to make herself over, to present the svelte kind of girl he was accustomed to before he woke up next to her. But he'd quickly put a stop to that, dragging her back to bed and making sweet love to her even when she was disheveled and uncombed.

"I told you before something was going on with him, and I think it just might be you."

She thought about that for a moment. Maybe Sophie was right. When they set the terms for this fling, Brad was hell bent on avoiding anything that resembled a relationship, but now, well, maybe like her he wanted more than just sex too. As she considered it further, she felt a small kernel of hope blossoming inside her. There was no denying that she was in love with Brad, had been for quite some time now. So maybe it really was time to put him to the test, to see if there could be more between him and the real Madison.

11

Darkness had fallen over the city as Brad pulled his truck into Madison's driveway and killed the ignition. He only just put the house up and still couldn't believe the realtor had found a buyer so fast. But the realtor had told him that a great house priced right, in the right area, always turned over fast. He glanced at the papers that he'd signed earlier, papers the new owners would be signing tonight and sealing the deal. He was happy to see a nice young couple buying it, but felt a strange sense of loss knowing he was parting with a big piece of his past, a place where he had many happy memories.

He glanced at the dashboard clock. Shit, he was running late. He'd planned to spend a few hours with Madison before he left tonight, but his meeting with the realtor had taken longer than he anticipated. If he wanted to make it to his drop-off point on the outskirts of town, he was going to have to speed to get there on time.

Just as he was about to climb from the cab, a text message came in. He fished his phone from his pocket and swiped his finger over the screen. He read the message from Jonah and learned that the convoy had arrived earlier than anticipated, but wouldn't be leaving again tonight due to maintenance issue. Brad's heart raced as he read it a second time. The delay meant he'd have another night, and morning, with Madison. If she wanted him, that is. Christ knew she'd reminded him of their deadline enough over the past thirty days.

He jumped from the truck, and used his key to let himself in, excitement building inside him to know she was upstairs waiting for him, and that he could take her into his arms one last time. Hurried footsteps carried him through the dark, downstairs bakery, and he rushed up the stairs, taking them two at a time.

"Madison," he called as he walked to her partially open door. He knocked gently, then called out to her again as he inched it open. "Madison, are you in here?"

"Brad," she said, her voice coming from behind.

He spun around, and his heart nearly failed when he saw her standing outside the bathroom door, looking more beautiful than ever. With her long hair tied back, showcasing a naturally beautiful face, she adjusted her glasses and met his gaze straight on. His eyes dropped to her comfy clothes, ones he'd missed seeing her in. As he perused them, his imagination kicked into high gear, thinking about all her sexy curves beneath those sweats, not to mention all the ways he could get her out of them.

"You're running late," she said, her voice sounding garbled through her bite plate.

As he stood there looking at her, loving that she was confident and comfortable enough to just be herself with him, everything he felt for her swept over him like a windstorm. His throat clenched, the muscles running along his chin tightening and contracting as his jaw seesawed from side to side.

"Brad?" she asked, her voice a hesitant whisper as she took two steps toward him. "Is everything okay?"

Hell no, everything was not okay. Barely able to draw in air, let alone speak as a flash of possessiveness whipped through him, he briefly closed his eyes, his mind racing, trying like hell to figure out what to say, what to do about the things he was feeling for her. The truth was, he hadn't felt this kind of connection in a long time. In fact he wasn't even certain he'd ever felt like this before. Sure he'd been engaged once, but oddly enough, with Madison it felt different. But before he could pull himself together, a knock sounded on the downstairs door.

He looked down the stairs and when he saw Jocelyn standing outside the front door, his stomach clenched. "Shit," he said, stepping past Madison. "I'll be right back."

He took the stairs two at a time, wondering what Jocelyn was doing here this time of night. She gave him a dazzling smile when he opened the door. "What can I do for you, Jocelyn?" he asked.

She pouted and lifted a suitcase. "I told you I'd see you again. To deliver your stuff, remember?" She went quiet for a moment then said, "And I thought we could talk."

He pitched his voice low. "I told you, we have nothing left to talk about."

With loneliness written all over her face, she went up on her toes, and ran her hands through his hair. "Come on, Brad. Don't be mad."

As he looked at her, he instantly realized he wasn't mad. Not anymore. In fact he felt nothing at all. No, that wasn't true. What he felt was sorry for her, because there really was a time when he cared about her, and now he really only wanted her to find happiness and true love, the way he had.

True love...

Jesus.

A noise behind him had him spinning around, and he found Madison standing at the foot of the stairs, watching the exchange. One look at her, all warm and cozy and waiting for him, and he knew he wanted this, all of this. She was beautiful on the outside as well as the inside and seeing her so comfortable with him, looking both homey and sexy at the same time nearly did him in.

He turned back to Jocelyn, and instantly knew it was time to let go of the past and move on. He'd been a fool to let old hurts stand in his way of what he wanted. After all, wasn't he a guy who fought for what he wanted, what was right, and what was worth fighting for? Deep in his heart he knew that was Madison.

Just then his grandfather's words came back to haunt him, and he shook his head. Jesus Christ, he really was dense. Why had it taken him so long to see that Madison was everything he'd ever wanted, inside the bedroom and out? Could his granddad have been right about Madison too? Had he been the boy she'd always wanted? He wasn't sure, but he was hell bent on making sure she knew he was the man for her now, because what he felt for her was real and completely over-whelming, in a good way. Loving her felt right, in his head and in his heart.

As a sense of belonging rolled over him, he thought about a conversation he once had with Madison. It was true, when he returned from away he wanted to come back to things that made him feel at home, things that made him feel happy. And he couldn't imagine coming home to anyone but the sweet and sexy girl who'd crawled past his defenses without even trying. Deep in his soul, he knew he didn't need to worry about betrayal. Not with her. She wasn't the type of girl to sleep around on him when he was away working. No, she was sweet and kind, the most compassionate and giving woman he knew, and it was damn well time to change her mind on this deadline they set in place, and prove to her that they belonged together.

But how?

His gut clenched, and as he thought about the papers the new owners were about to sign, the future he so desperately wanted slipping from his fingers, he looked at Madison and blurted out, "I have to go."

"I know," she murmured, hugging her arms around her body. "You're running late."

He pushed past Jocelyn, and she chatted endlessly as she followed him to his truck. He pulled open his door, but before he got in, he turned to her, put his hands on her shoulders and softened his voice when he said, "I hope you find what you're looking for, Jocelyn, but I think we both know it's not me."

She went quiet for a moment, glanced at the bakery door, then back at him. She exhaled slowly and nodded. "I'm sorry, Brad."

"I know, and I also know you'll find someone who will make you happy."

Hope lit her eyes and his heart softened for her. "Do you think so?"

"I know so. You take care of yourself, okay?"

She nodded. "You too."

With that, Brad dropped a soft kiss onto her forehead and climbed into his truck.

With single-minded determination, he turned the ignition over, and backed down the driveway, determined to stop this deal from going through. His very future depended on it.

———

Madison's heart pounded so hard against her ribcage as she watched Brad leave, she thought it would burst from her chest. She hurried back upstairs, but when she tripped over his military bag, she stilled, her mind searching for answers. If he wasn't rushing off to catch his convoy, why then had he run out of her place so fast, leaving his gear behind?

God, could she have been so wrong about him? Had one glimpse of the real Madison sent him into the arms of his ex? She swallowed, refusing to believe that about him, especially after seeing the way he looked at her earlier. There was so much desire and passion in his eyes that it weakened her knees and had her heart turning over in her chest. Everything in the way he looked at her, told her he wanted so much more too. So why then, did he bolt from her place like he was on fire?

With her emotions in a confused mess, she walked aimlessly around her bedroom, exhaustion pulling at her as she tried to figure out what was going on. She sat on the edge of her bed, but when she caught Brad's scent, she knew she could never spend the night in here, especially if he had no intention of ever coming back to her.

As a yawn pulled at her, the pain medication she'd taken earlier wiping her out, she thought about stripping the mattress and washing the sheets, but decided against it. Instead, she pulled on her knee-length nightshirt and made her way down the hall. At least in Jonah's room she wouldn't be bombarded with memories of all the erotic things she and Brad had done in hers.

She pulled back the sheets and climbed inside, missing Brad's warmth as she desperately tried to figure out what was going on inside that head of his. She quieted her mind and thought things through, recalling the way Brad had been so tender and caring with her, helping her overcome her body image issues to become confident in herself, confident enough to present the side of her that got her teased in high school.

Then another thought hit. Perhaps Brad was still harboring anger over his ex, still too afraid to put his heart on the line and try again. And perhaps when Jocelyn had knocked on the door, the sight of her brought back too many painful memories, and had him running in the opposite direction.

Maybe it was time for her to help him move past his issues, because he was a good man, one who deserved what he always wanted. And damned if she wasn't the girl to give it to him. She let loose a breath and snuggled into the sheets, ever determined to make this work between them, because she believed in him, and she believed in herself.

12

Brad sped through the city streets, taking the corners too fast and running the lights when no other vehicles were around. He pulled up in front of Grand-dad's beautiful old homestead and when he saw two cars in the driveway his heart went to his throat.

He jumped from the cab of his truck, ripped the *For Sale* sign off the lawn and ran into the house. When he stepped inside and three sets of eyes turned his way, he blurted out, "It's not for sale."

"Brad," his realtor said, jumping from his seat at the small round kitchen table, "What's going on?"

Brad looked at the young couple who'd put in an offer earlier that day, their eyes wide and confused as they sat at the oak table talking about the house with his realtor. "I made a mistake. The house is no longer for sale."

Disappointment moved over the young woman's face as her glance went from Brad, to the realtor, to her husband. "But I thought—"

"I'm sorry, I just can't sell it."

"I think you're too late, pal," the guy said, his voice challenging as he stood up. "You accepted our offer and already signed the papers."

"No, you don't understand. I can't sell it."

The man folded his arm over a broad chest, but his wife stood beside him and put her hand on his arm. Her brow furrowed. "What's going on?"

Brad scrubbed his fingers through his hair. "This house... it's my future...my....everything."

"Brad," the realtor said in a soft tone voice meant to placate. "You're not making any sense."

"Look," he blurted out. "I'm in love. So fucking crazy in love I don't know what to do with myself. And I want to show her just how much I love her, by giving her what she's always wanted."

"What has she always wanted?" the girl asked.

"A house...a family...in the right neighborhood. One she can live in forever, and turn the downstairs into a bakery." He pointed to the wrap around deck that he could close in and turn into an eating area. "This place is the perfect location for Sweetie's Bakery. The perfect house for her...for us."

"Sweetie's Bakery?" the girl asked, her eyes wide. "Are you talking about Madison Graham?"

Brad nodded, his heart beating so hard in his chest he felt dizzy. "Yeah, do you know her?"

"Not personally, but I eat at her bakery all the times. She's amazing."

"Yeah, she is amazing."

The woman looked at her husband, who seemed to be shifting uneasily on his feet. "We can't buy this place now," the petite blonde said.

"Yeah, I knew you were going to say that." He shrugged and held a hand out to Brad. "What can I say, I'm a sucker for love too."

"Thank you." Brad rushed out, and after a quick handshake he darted into the small office to grab the blueprints he'd been working off of while refinishing the place. He had one more stop to make before he hurried back to Madison.

Three long hours later, after waking his friend and putting him to work on modifying the blueprints to incorporate a downstairs café, he was back in his truck on his way to see Madison, equal amounts of excitement and nervousness erupting in the pit of his gut.

He drove into her parking lot and noted that all the lights were out. Assuming she'd gone to bed, after all she probably thought he'd be on his way up north at this point, he unlocked the door and quietly stepped inside.

The steps groaned under his weight as he walked upstairs, but when he reached her bedroom and found it empty, worry moved through him. Where the hell was she?

Turning around, he made his way down the hall toward the bathroom, but when a noise inside Jonah's room caught his attention, he pushed the door open. What he saw next stopped his heart and had all his blood draining to his feet.

The blueprints fell from his hands, and when the tube hit the floor, Madison sat up and rubbed her eyes.

"Brad?" she asked. "What?" She paused and pulled out her bite plate to talk. "What's going on?"

"What the hell?" Jonah said, from his side of the bed. "Brad?" Jonah flicked the light on, and Brad's glance went from the woman he loved, to the brother who'd stolen his women more times than enough. "What the fuck?" Jonah asked, scratching his head as he blinked against the bright light.

Brad shook his head, and if he didn't know better, he'd say his brother really had taken over where he left off.

"Brad," Madison said breathlessly. "It's not what you think."

Brad straightened. "Oh, no. I think it's exactly what I think."

Madison flung the bed sheets off and moved toward him. His heart pounded with everything he felt for her as she smoothed her hands over her long nightshirt. The same one she'd transformed into a prize winning T-shirt a month ago, when they started their affair. An affair that changed everything between them.

"Brad, please," she said, panic in her voice as stopped at the foot of the bed. "Let me explain."

"Madison—"

She pointed to Jonah shifting uneasily in the bed behind her, then toward her bedroom at the end of the hall. "I forgot...I didn't want to sleep...I didn't know if you were coming back."

He pulled her to him and wrapped his arms around her waist. "You don't have to explain anything, Madison."

"I don't."

"No. I trust you."

Worry left her face. "You do?"

"Yes."

"Then where did you go? Why did you run out on me like that?"

"Because the second I saw you standing outside the bathroom earlier tonight, looking so warm and comfortable with me, I knew I wanted to make this arrangement between us permanent."

"You do?" she asked, her breath coming quicker.

"Yeah, and I wanted to show you how much I care." He bent down and grabbed the blueprints. He pulled them from the tube and spread them open to show her the changes on the house. When he looked back at her tears were in her eyes.

"Madison," he began, "I know you were counting down the thirty days, but I don't want this to end."

"I was only counting down the days because I figured I could only keep up the façade that long."

"Façade?"

"Yeah, I've seen the women you gravitate toward, and well, I knew I could be that kind of woman for a short time." She waved her hand over her clothes. "But eventually this side of me would show through."

"Babe," he said, "I love how you've grown comfortable in your skin, but I love this side of you too. This is the side that made me realize I wanted you in my life forever."

He listened to her throat work as she gulped. "Forever?"

"Yes, forever. I want us to live in this house together, raise a family together." When she went quiet, he exhaled sharply. "Jesus, Madison, please tell me you want that too."

Her hand touched his cheek, her touch so soft, so intimate, so full of emotion. She smiled up at him, and his heart stopped because he recognized that look, it was the same one he'd seen Tallulah give Garrett, the same one she'd given him when he pulled her back to bed that morning so long ago, when he refused to let her rush from his arms to freshen up.

"You love me," he said, a statement, not a question.

"Yes, Brad. I love you. I've always loved you. Ever since we were kids, I've loved you."

His heart took flight, and he was sure he was grinning like the village idiot when he shook his head and said, "Jesus, I had no idea."

Her smile widened and there was so much love on her face as she looked up at him that it took his breath away. She poked a finger into his chest. "That's because your granddad was right."

His head came back with a start. "About what?"

She chuckled. "Sometimes you can be really dense."

When Brad laughed with her, Jonah flung his covers off and jackknifed in the bed. "What the fuck is going on?"

Brad shifted his focus, so lost in Madison that he'd forgotten Jonah was there. "What's going on is I'm in love with Madison, and I want her to be my wife."

Jonah gave a hard shake of his head. "One month. I've been gone for one fucking month and the world goes to hell around me!"

"The world hasn't gone to hell, Jonah. The world is just how it should be, how it should have been a long time ago." He looked at Madison. "So what do you say, Madison? Will you marry me, move into the house with me and start that family we both always wanted, while we turn the downstairs into a bakery?"

"One condition," she said.

He angled his head. "Condition?"

"When I'm in the kitchen, you let me wear my apron."

With that he laughed out loud, scooped her up and carried her to her bedroom, where he spent the rest of the night buried inside the woman he loved with all his heart. A woman who helped him let go of the past and taught him to love again.

Jesus, those had to be the biggest melons he'd ever set eyes on.

Security expert Luke Phillips swallowed down the saliva pooling on his tongue and stared at the gorgeous woman coming his way. With his mouth watering for a taste of those juicy, oversized melons, his gaze traveled upward to meet with a set of big blue eyes that held a measure of panic.

"Shit," he mumbled, and discarded his cart to help. It wasn't like he'd actually planned on purchasing any of the groceries inside, anyway. No, like any good thief, he was simply pretending to be a customer when all the while he was actually scoping out the place. Seconds before the woman's armload of honeydews went crashing to the floor, Luke quickly closed the distance between them and reached out to help her.

"Here, let me lighten your load." His cock twitched. Okay, wrong choice of words...

She stopped dead in her tracks, her dark lashes blinking rapidly in confusion as she stared up at him. His head came back with a start, surprised by her reaction. What, had she never been offered help before?

"It's okay, I got it." She arched her back as she awkwardly shifted the gigantic fruits before they fell and splattered on the polished tile floor.

Ignoring her protest, he grabbed three melons, leaving her with two, and glanced at the nametag pinned to her apron. *Emery*. Different, but pretty. Like her.

"Now what kind of guy would I be if I just stood here watching you juggle your melons?" He tossed her his best flirtatious grin trying to make light of the situation and put a smile on her face.

"Thanks," she mumbled, but instead of playing along, she gestured with a nod to the table set up at the end of the grocery aisle. *Tough crowd*. "You can put them there. But just so you know, I did have everything under control." She jutted her chin out a little bit, and Luke's grin widened as she tried to hold her own against him.

"Are you always this stubborn?" He took in the curves her work apron did little to hide. Stubborn, yet sexy. Damned if she wasn't his kind of girl.

She shook her head and loose blonde curls flared around her shoulders. He breathed in the floral fragrance of her shampoo, pulling it deep into his lungs as it overshadowed the scent of ripe honeydew.

"I'm not... I just... Look, I'm just in a hurry, that's all." She placed the melons on the table, adjusted the sale sign, then glanced at her watch. "I have to be somewhere in ten minutes."

He took in the worry in her eyes and the pink tinge on her cheeks before he stole a peek at his own watch. At twelve noon he too had to be somewhere. Not that he had far to go. No, his meeting was with the owner of the upscale market smack dab in the middle of Austin's trendiest neighborhood

—a market he never, ever thought he'd step foot in again. If it weren't for the youth who hung out at Sheffield Community Center, he'd have stayed as far away from the place as possible. But he'd promised the kids new equipment and since he never went back on his word, he had no choice but to take the job. That, and the owner was now a woman, which had him thinking Taylor's Market had changed hands in the last decade. Yeah, he was pretty certain the man who fought to put the "kid from the wrong side of the tracks" in juvenile detention—and won—had retired and was long gone from the place.

"I'm no efficiency expert, but more hands make lighter work." He followed her back to the pile of melons she was moving, and assuming she had to rush off to some appointment on her lunch break, he added, "Shouldn't you get one of the other staff members to help if you have to be out of here in ten?"

Something troubled passed over her pretty eyes as she grabbed another armload and shifted them in the crook of her elbow. She pinched her lips tight, then said, "We're short staffed."

Of course they were, which was probably why the owner, Mrs. Vincent, had called his company looking for a security expert in the first place. Overworked staff had a negative impact on employee health, leading to shortages due to stress-related illnesses. It also had a negative impact on the business itself. With no one watching the store, a thief could easily rob Taylor's Market blind—and likely had—considering they were looking for his services.

Luke had come to the market early to get a feel for their security, and as he stole another glance around, he could see why they needed his help. The place was packed with customers, and there were only three employees on the floor: Emery working produce, a young man behind the deli counter, and one cashier working the front register. Unfortunately, there was no management to be found. Not that Luke thought management would ever help a lowly employee. God forbid anyone in the upper echelons get their hands dirty.

Or give second chances...

But they should at least be watching the store and monitoring the place for theft.

He helped her carry another armload, finishing off the stack, and took note of a young boy around fourteen years old combing the aisles. From the way his T-shirt jutted out from his baggy jeans, it was easy to tell the kid had a pocketful of stolen goods. Luke exhaled slowly, memories of his own youth bombarding him as he kept watchful eyes on the little delinquent. The kid glanced at him, made eye contact, then moved to the next aisle.

Even though Luke wasn't officially on the job yet, he placed the last of the melons on the display table, knowing he had to do something. Stepping into soldier mode he excused himself and walked to the front of the store. He had every intention of catching up with her later to get her number.

He stood by the door and once again took in all the holes in the store's security system as he waited for the kid to exit. Even though it was nearing his appointment time, he wanted to deal with the boy first. At least if he was the one doling out the punishment the kid stood half a chance. Painful past experiences had taught him that the rich lived by their own rules and were biased against those outside their elite circle.

When he saw the boy round an aisle and sidestep the long line at the cash register, Luke picked up a box of specialty cookies and pretended to study the ingredients, giving the boy a chance to escape. For his plan to work, he needed to catch the kid red-handed, outside the store.

The boy slipped out the door. Luke put the box down and followed. He walked behind him for a few seconds, moisture breaking out on his forehead as the warm sunshine heated the sidewalk and radiated upward.

He closed the gap, and when he was within arm's reach he said, "Hey."

The boy spun around, and his eyes went wide with recognition as Luke glared at him. "What the fuck do you want, man?"

Nice...

Luke gestured with a nod. "How about everything in your pockets."

"Shit." The kid cursed and turned to run. Since Luke had anticipated the boy's next move he was already one step ahead of him and had him by the scruff before he could round the corner and bolt.

Luke turned him around and nudged him toward the market, hoping to find a quiet place inside. "How about we have a little talk?"

"How about you go fuck yourself."

"That's a nice mouth you've got there," Luke said. "Do you kiss your mother good night with it?"

"I kiss lots of girls with it." He smirked and struggled against Luke's grip, but this wasn't Luke's first rodeo. In fact, a little over a decade ago, many of his friends had stood where the boy was right now—and Luke had spent three years in juvenile detention because of it.

Luke practically dragged him inside and when he found a handful of customers staring at him, he searched for Emery. The commotion must have caught her attention. She rushed from the back of the store and when she saw him with the struggling boy, her eyes went wide.

"Is there an office around here I can use for a minute?" Luke asked.

"What's going on?"

"What's going on is this kid has a pocket full of goods."

"Oh, I didn't…" When she pushed her curls from her face, Luke noticed a worried frown creasing her forehead. She pointed toward the back. "I was busy. I didn't see."

"It's fine. I've got it under control," Luke explained, not wanting her to think the blame was hers. It was management's job to train the staff and put theft prevention measures in place.

"Are you a cop?" she asked.

"Something like that." The kid elbowed Luke in the gut and Luke tensed. "About that room," he said between gritted teeth.

She nodded and he followed her to the back of the store. She pulled a ring full of keys from her pocket and unlocked the door with shaky fingers. Luke stepped past her and she followed him. Once inside the small office, Luke shoved the kid into a chair and leaned against the desk, taking an authoritative, high-powered position over him, a tactic he'd learned in the army. Emery stood by the door, looking completely unsure of herself—of Luke—and the situation she'd suddenly found herself in. Luke could have told her to leave, but he needed her there for two reasons. One, she would be a witness to what he was about to do, and two, he was a selfish prick and liked being around her. And of course, he couldn't forget that he'd yet to get her number.

"What's your name?" Luke asked the boy, lowering his voice slightly.

"Captain America," the kid responded with a smirk.

Luke let that statement stand for a while as he assessed the boy. One thing was for sure, he wasn't as tough as he wanted Luke to think he was. He took in his ratty shirt, jeans that were two sizes too big, and sneakers that had seen better days. As the puzzle known as Captain America clicked together, Luke felt his heart pinch, but he kept his face hard, his voice deep.

"So what are you, some kind of street thug?"

The kid slouched in his chair, his nonchalant body language belying the worry backlighting his dark eyes. As a former military security specialist, Luke knew all about reading people, and despite trying to appear unfazed, the kid was scared shitless. Which meant Luke had him right where he wanted him. If the kid really was a badass, there was no way Luke could get him to agree to the terms he was about to lay out.

Captain American folded his arms—a protective measure to shield himself, and a sure sign of his anxiety. "Yeah, that's what I am," he answered. "A street thug with superpowers."

Luke gave him his best hard-assed glare and stared at him for longer than was comfortable. Eventually the boy shifted, straightening slightly in his seat. Good. At least somewhere deep inside he still held a degree of respect for authority and wasn't a lost cause.

Luke met his gaze unflinchingly. "Did someone put you up to this?"

After a long moment, the boy tore his gaze away and stared at his sneakers, ending the uncomfortable stare down. "Here, just take the stuff." He reached into his pocket and pulled out two pieces of red licorice and tossed them onto the desk.

"You don't seem like a stupid kid." Luke picked up the candy and slapped it against his palm. Behind the boy's nervousness he had a solid determination about him, an intelligence that ran deep. "In fact, I'd say you're pretty smart, which makes me wonder why you're willing to ruin your life for two pieces of licorice."

"I'm not... I didn't... I don't..." He pushed agitated fingers through dark, shoulder-length hair that looked like it hadn't been shampooed in weeks.

"This can go down one of two ways," Luke began. "I call

in backup and you end up in juvie for stealing..." He paused to give the kid a moment to chew on that, even though he had no intention of ever calling the cops.

"Fuck," the boy mumbled, his voice cracking slightly. "Look, the licorice wasn't even for me."

"So someone did put you up to this."

He stared at the floor, and fisted his hair. "It's for my little brother, okay? He likes licorice."

"Your little brother?"

"Yeah, he's only three and doesn't get..." He stopped talking, like he didn't want to give away too much.

"What else do you have in your pockets?" The boy hesitated, and Luke reached for the phone.

"Okay, fine." He pulled out a tube of deli meats and slapped it on the table.

Luke picked up the package and exchanged a look with Emery. Troubled eyes full of mixed emotions stared back, a clear sign that she knew what was going on. Taylor's Market might have been in Austin's trendiest neighborhood, but just a few blocks away things went south fast. Luke knew first-hand what it was like to live in the city's poverty district, where food and candy were hard to come by.

"Is this for your brother too?" he asked, keeping his face hard. A kid like Captain America here would never want his pity.

"Yeah." He emptied his other pocket and placed a couple of crusty rolls on the desk. "So what's the other way?"

"The other way?" Luke asked.

"You said this could go down one of two ways."

"The other way is you spend every weekend this summer at the community center out in Sheffield."

"Fuck. Isn't that where old people hang out?"

Old people, young people, therapy dogs. Luke picked the phone up.

"Don't. I'll do it," the boy said. Luke continued to glare at him, waiting for a stronger reaction. The boy cursed under his breath, held his hands up, palms out. "I'll do it, okay. Just put the damn phone down."

Luke took his hand off the receiver. "Get up, kid."

The boy stood. "It's Trent, and I'm not a kid."

"Okay, Trent," he began, giving him that much, despite the fact that he *was* a kid—one who not only needed, but was craving guidance in the worst way. "Where do you live?"

He narrowed suspicious eyes. "Why?"

"Because I'm going to walk you home so I'll know where to find you if you don't show up on Saturday."

"Fine," he mumbled.

After he gave the address, Luke nudged him toward the door, but didn't miss Emery jotting the address down on a whiteboard hung near the desk. For a moment he thought she might report him, but he'd seen the look in her eyes. She felt for the kid every bit as much as Luke did. "And don't think you're getting off easy. Juvie might look like a day in the park after a weekend at the center."

He moved to the door and the sweet floral scent of Emery hit him as she stood there nibbling her bottom lip, looking at him with an equal mixture of worry and relief. "Listen, will you tell the owner that I'll be late for my appointment?"

As if a light bulb had just gone off, her big eyes went wide. She shook her head, her long curls bouncing around her shoulders. "You're...you're Mr. Phillips...from..." Her words fell off and she finished with, "I should have known."

He stopped dead in his tracks and took a moment to look at her. She really was gorgeous, but there was something in her eyes that told him she wore the weight of the world on her shoulders. Damned if he didn't want to help lighten that load too.

"Yeah. I'm Luke Phillips, from Phillips Security." He gave

her a **suggestive** smile, along with a teasing wink, determined to **loosen her up** and put a smile on that lush mouth of hers. He pitched his voice low, for her ears only and said, "Which **means I'll be** hanging out here for the next few weeks and while I'm here, you'll never again have to juggle your melons alone."

Emery Vincent tried to quiet her racing heart as she watched Mr. Phillips, or rather Luke-o-licious, escort the boy from her office. Surprised that her legs could actually move, she crossed the small tile floor and plopped herself down in her old leather chair, her mind racing with this unexpected turn of events. When she'd called Phillips Security and talked to his receptionist, she expected a hardened soldier to show up, not sex in a formfitting T-shirt.

You'll never again have to juggle your melons alone.

Oh, God!

He'd been teasing her, flirting with her, but she'd been too focused on her upcoming meeting—on losing the business her ailing father had left her in hands—to partake in his sexy banter.

Unable to help herself she stole a glance at him as he walked down the deli aisle with delinquent Trent in tow. As she thanked her lucky stars that he was good at his job and had stopped one more theft, she took in his long, hard legs and low-slung jeans that cradled his backside to perfection—and oh what a backside it was.

After a good, long look, her gaze traveled up to take in a wide back and even wider shoulders. She caught a glimpse of his tattoo peeking out from the short sleeves of his T-shirt, and her fingers itched to explore the rest of him to see if he had any more ink. She continued to stare, unable to help herself, but when he turned back and caught her ogling, he gave her a sexy, lopsided smile—one that spoke of hot nights and even hotter sex.

Oh my...

Okay, so she totally knew what his teasing was all about. The man wanted her between the sheets. Hell, who was she kidding? She wanted that too. The last time she'd crawled into bed with a guy was a little over two years ago. That lust-affair hadn't ended well. Then again, for as long as she could remember, none of her relationships ever had. In kinder-garten no one wanted to play with the girl who had a "retarded" brother, as they called him, because they thought it might rub off. God, kids were so damn cruel, twisting that clinical word to make it so ugly and offensive when all it really meant was that he had special needs. It was wrong to call people names, any kind of name. Simple as that.

In Emery's later years, kids started talking to her when they found out her folks ran the market. They befriended her, only to score free candy and soda in their middle school years, and alcohol and smokes in their later ones—which she ended up paying for.

She'd learned the hard way that people hung out with her for one reason and one reason only—they wanted something. And that something was never a lifelong friendship, or a lasting romantic love affair, like she really wanted.

From his outwardly flirtatious personality, she assumed Luke was a player, which was fine by her. She wasn't opposed to a night of sex with a hot guy like him—no strings attached. Hey, at least her eyes were wide open and she knew never to trust, never to set herself up for failure. And, hell, a night in the sack would undoubtedly help ease the tension that had been building inside her since taking over the business two years ago—and watching it go downhill. Things had been good for the first year, but then over the last twelve months she started losing thousands of dollars every pay period. With an expanding neighborhood, and a busier store, she chalked the losses up to theft, but lack of cash flow meant she had to lay off employees. Less staff meant fewer people to watch the store, which only compounded the problem.

She exhaled slowly, her mind going back to Luke and the reason she'd called his company in the first place. From his teasing banter she guessed he had no idea she was the owner of the market. She'd always gone by Vincent-Taylor and had dropped the Taylor from her last name a few years ago, keeping her mother's name only. Partly to honor her after she died, and partly because, well, everyone wanted something from a Taylor. Her father had numerous connections in high places, and many favors were traded. Emery just wanted people to like her for who she was, not for what she could give them—or do for them.

Regardless, now was not the time to be thinking about that, not when her father had trusted her with the business and she needed to make it a success not only for him, but also for her older brother. The residential health facility where he received around-the-clock nursing care was expensive, but it was also the best facility in the state, and she wasn't about to jeopardize his well-being due to lack of funds. He was counting on her and she wouldn't let him down, which meant all her focus had to go into saving the market.

She took a crisp twenty-dollar bill from her purse and jotted Trent's address down on a sticky note. Pushing to her feet, she made her way into the market with the product Luke had left on her desk.

Luke...

Hot, hard, so nice to look at. She thought about the way he'd shifted gears with Trent, and in seconds flat had gone from flirtatious to deadly serious. She'd caught the intense glint in his steel-gray eyes as he hardened himself, and suspected there was more to him than met the eye. Beneath all the charm and charisma she suspected that ex-soldier Luke Phillips had a past that continued to haunt him. Behind the charming grin, and flirty smile, there was a darker part of him.

Even still, her body was screaming at her to cut loose and have some much-needed fun with the guy who oozed sex. But she had a business to fix, she reminded herself. Which meant she needed to concentrate on running the market, and not on what her body craved.

Then again, look how that had turned out for her.

Yeah, some inner voice yelled—probably the one calling the shots from between her legs—*look where that got you. Go ahead, have some fun with Luke-o-licious. Let him juggle your melons. You know you want to.*

ABOUT CATHRYN

New York Times and *USA today* Bestselling author, Cathryn is a wife, mom, sister, daughter, and friend. She loves dogs, sunny weather, anything chocolate (she never says no to a brownie) pizza and red wine. She has two teenagers who keep her busy with their never ending activities, and a husband who is convinced he can turn her into a mixed martial arts fan. Cathryn can never find balance in her life, is always trying to find time to go to the gym, can never keep up with emails, Facebook or Twitter and tries to write page-turning books that her readers will love.

Connect with Cathryn:
Newsletter
https://app.mailerlite.com/webforms/landing/c1f8n1
Twitter: https://twitter.com/writercatfox
Facebook:
https://www.facebook.com/AuthorCathrynFox?ref=hl
Blog: http://cathrynfox.com/blog/
Goodreads:
https://www.goodreads.com/author/show/91799.Cathryn_Fox

Pinterest http://www.pinterest.com/catkalen/

Hands On

Body Contact

Full Exposure

Dossier

Private Reserve

House Rules

Under Pressure

Big Catch

Brazilian Fantasy

Improper Proposal

Boys of Beachville

Good at Being Bad

Igniting the Bad Boy

Bad Girl Therapy

Stone Cliff Series:

Crashing Down

Wasted Summer

Love Lessons

Wrapped Up

Eternal Pleasure Series

Instinctive

Impulsive

Indulgent

Sun Stroked Series

Seaside Seduction

Deep Desire

Private Pleasure

Captured and Claimed Series:

Yours to Take

Yours to Teach

Yours to Keep

Firefighter Heat Series

Fever

Siren

Flash Fire

Playing For Keeps Series

Slow Ride

Wild Ride

Sweet Ride

Breaking the Rules:

Hold Me Down Hard

Pin Me Up Proper

Tie Me Down Tight

Stand Alone Title:

Hands on with the CEO

Torn Between Two Brothers

Holiday Spirit

Unleashed

Knocking on Demon's Door

Web of Desire